Angie

Bruce Collier

STRATTON
—PRESS—
Publishing Life

Angie
Copyright © 2019 **Bruce Collier**

Stratton Press Publishing
831 N Tatnall Street Suite M #188,
Wilmington, DE 19801
www.stratton-press.com
1-888-323-7009

ISBN (Paperback): 978-1-64345-581-5
ISBN (Ebook): 978-1-64345-689-8

Printed in the United States of America

CHAPTER 1

In her small dingy bedroom, sitting on the edge of a worn-out bed that should have been discarded many years before, thirteen-year-old Angela Blake was trying to recover from a shocking experience. What she had witnessed a few minutes earlier was fixed in her mind, and even though the picture was clear, she could not believe what she had seen.

In her lap, holding it with both hands, was her most cherished possession—a picture of her father. She raised his face close to hers, kissed the tear-covered glass, then licked her cold, wet lips as she searched his face and eyes for answers to questions she had asked many times before.

"Why, Dad?" she asked out loud. "Why did you have to die? And why did Mom marry such a creep?" She wrapped her arms around the frame and caressed it close to her chest. "I hate Mom! And I really hate John." She pressed her cheek against the top of the frame and tightened her embrace. "I miss you so much."

Angie and her father had been extremely close, closer than most fathers and daughters, which, in Angie's opinion, caused her mother to resent the time he spent with her and the affection he showed. Angie's mother had never expressed any affection—not to Angie or her father; she only criticized, ridiculed, and complained. There had been many times when Angie made an effort to get close to her mother, but her attempts were always unsuccessful; the embarrassing, cruel, sarcastic remarks she had to endure made her regret that she even tried.

Not long before her father's accident, she heard him ask her mother why she always seemed to resent Angie's efforts to be close.

"She's not sincere. She's faking" was her answer. After hearing what her mother said, Angie lost what little respect she had for her and, from that day on, tried to avoid any contact. Unfortunately, her desire to distance herself from her mother created even more friction between them, and now that her father was no longer there to protect her, the abuse she suffered was much worse, especially the mental abuse. But nothing compared to what she had just witnessed.

After her shower, she had gone in the living room to ask her mother a question; her mother must have assumed she was still in the shower. A sharp pain seized Angie's stomach; one hand rushed to comfort it, while the other hand covered her open mouth. What was happening was too obvious to miss. Her mother was sitting on the edge of the sofa; John was standing in front of her with his pants down. Instead of being shocked when she saw Angie, she calmly stopped, looked at her, and said, "Oh well," then returned to what she was doing.

Dazed and bewildered, Angie turned and ran to her room.

The image of her mother and John was like the flash of a camera, only a glimpse, but a picture as clear as a photograph, and one that would last just as long.

Still holding her father's picture, she lay back on her bed and tried to concentrate on the grimy ceiling. No matter how much she focused on the peeling paint, the dusty light fixture, and the spider webs in the corners—all yellow from years of cigarette smoke—she could not erase the nonchalant look on her mother's face when she pulled away from John or the lack of compassion in her voice when she said "Oh well."

Several times before, Angie had accidentally walked in on her mother having sex with other men, but this was the first time with John and the first time she had witnessed anything as shocking or as disturbing. She wondered if what she had experienced was just a sample of what she could expect while living in John's small trailer.

Angie

The last two years had been extremely difficult for Angie—her father's death being the most traumatic. He was on his way home from his second job when he ran off the road and hit a tree. The police said he must've fallen asleep; working two jobs had taken its toll. He took the second job to pay off the credit card debts her mother had accumulated.

Angie had never seen her father express the anger he did the night he discovered her mother had maxed out all their credit cards. She watched as her father removed the cards from her mother's wallet.

"I can't believe the mess you've gotten us in," he said as he held them in his left hand and shuffled the top card to the bottom, over and over, as if he were saying goodbye to some dear friends. After several minutes of doing this, he opened his desk drawer, took out a pair of scissors, and cut them in half. That was two months before his accident.

There had been many times, by making up lies, Angie's mother tried to come between Angie and her father, but fortunately, he recognized her selfish actions and resented her comments. Her mother's maneuvers only resulted in him having less respect for her and drew him closer to his daughter. Because of the friction between her father and mother, Angie suspected that if he had lived, they would have divorced.

Unfortunately, after his death, her mother went back to her old ways. She spent the insurance money, was fired from her job, lost their car and their home—all in less than two years.

Not long before they were forced to move from their home, Angie's mother met John, who, like her, was an alcoholic and unemployed. When Angie and her mother had no place to live, they moved in with John. Now, instead of the nice home her father had provided, they lived in a small filthy two-bedroom mobile home in one of the few bad areas of Bradenton, Florida. A few days after they moved in, John and her mother were married. They had lived with John for only six days, but to Angie, it seemed like six weeks.

Angie slowly lifted her father's picture from her chest and looked into his fixed eyes that would forever express his love. As she looked at his small smile, the same smile that always seemed to be there when they were together, she tried to think of the good times they shared, but the thought of her mother with John was too strong. She kissed his picture, as she did every night before turning her light off and every morning when she woke. She held it and slept with it the rest of the night.

As usual, Angie was dressed and ready for school before her mother was out of bed. She fixed her normal breakfast, a bowl of cereal, then sat at the small table in the kitchen area. The table was extremely dirty and scarred from years of cigarettes being placed along the edge and left to burn themselves out, as was every other piece of furniture John owned with an edge flat enough to hold a cigarette. A few days earlier, she tried to clean it, but the stains were too deep.

Hoping to be gone before John got up, she hurried to finish her cereal, but she didn't make it. She felt sick, too sick to eat. She looked up—John was standing in front of her.

With his eyes fixed on hers, he lifted his cigarette to his lips, inhaled deeply, then blew the smoke out the corner of his mouth, filling the room with smoke.

Not knowing what to expect, she kept her eyes on his and watched as he pulled out the chair across from her.

He slouched in the chair with his legs stretched out in front, his feet almost touching hers. Without moving his eyes from hers, he removed the cigarette, tilted his head back, and blew the smoke up and away from her, as if he were being considerate. Then, while smiling his yellow-teeth smile, he asked, "What'd you think of what you saw last night?"

She stood, took her bowl to the nasty sink, rinsed it, slammed the door behind her, and left without saying a word. *God, I hate him!*

Where she lived before, she walked to school. Now she had to take the bus. She didn't mind the bus ride; it was the kids at the bus stop she was uncomfortable with. Her clothes were way too small, which caused the boys to stare at her breasts and bottom and make rude, suggestive remarks; the girls laughed and pointed. Conditions at school were not much better.

It had been well over a year since her mother bought her anything new. She had matured considerably, but her mother refused to buy her a bra. She was told she would have to wait until she stopped growing. To keep her breasts from accidentally being exposed, she always had extra safety pins, just in case one or more buttons popped loose.

Normally, she tried to time her arrival at the bus stop to be the same as the bus, but she was early. She preferred to listen to the kids' cruel remarks and tolerate their stares than stay another minute in that small trailer with John.

It's bad enough that he brushes himself against me and purposely touches my breasts while reaching around me for something, but sitting at that dirty table, in that small room, listening to his crude remarks would have been impossible.

When John "accidentally" felt her breasts or her bottom, she had looked to her mother for help. His groping was far too obvious to miss, but her mother always acted as if she was unaware of what was happening. When Angie complained, she was accused of trying to cause trouble and was told that John would never do something like that. Angie felt helpless and alone when she realized her mother had chosen to believe whatever John did was accidental. She had decided that since she could not count on her mother for help, she would do her best to avoid him.

The thin wall separating their bedrooms was another condition Angie found difficult to deal with. She could hear every sound coming from their room, and it seemed there was no effort made to conceal their vulgar pleasures. It was as if they felt she enjoyed listening to the sounds of their sexual activities and gross comments. Most nights, they were so loud that Angie covered her head with her pillow, which was little help.

Even though the sounds were disgusting, there were times, on some of their quieter nights, she found them stimulating. On those nights, she lay awake and wondered when she would fall in love—and make love. She was convinced that instead of being like her mother, who had sex with just about any man, she was going to wait for love.

⁓

A few nights after the living room incident, Angie couldn't sleep. John and her mother's voices were loud and keeping her awake. Her mother's words were slurred as she refused John's suggestions; she seemed to be more intoxicated than usual. Listening to John's pleas and knowing they were arguing brought a smile to Angie; she wondered who would be victorious. When John tired of being rejected, his voice became loud and more demanding. Angie's curiosity quickly changed to fear when she heard her mother say, "Go see if Angie will take care of your needs."

Angie couldn't believe what her mother said and thought she had to be kidding. Her heart was pounding hard, so hard she felt her chest move with each beat.

The floor creaked. She kept hoping to hear her mother say she was only kidding, but there was only silence. By the squeaking sound of her door, she knew it was opening. She lay perfectly still, too afraid to move. What was happening was unimaginable; she felt she had to be dreaming. The door continued to squeak, stopped, started again, then closed. After hearing her mother's comment, she had turned off the nightlight she usually kept on; her eyes had not adjusted to the dark, and she wondered if he was in her room.

She felt as if she had been shocked by a powerful jolt of electricity when she heard, "Look what I have for you."

There was just enough moonlight coming in her window to see his nude body standing by her bed. Her racing heart felt as if it were going to beat right out of her chest—she didn't move. She felt him pull back her covers, then smelled the hot, rancid fumes coming from his filthy body as he lay beside her. Again, she didn't move, pretending to be sound asleep. She wished she wasn't pretending and would wake and see that he really wasn't there. Unfortunately, she knew he was.

She regretted that to make more room in her tiny bedroom, she had shoved her bed against the wall. Now she was trapped between him and the wall, the foot of the bed being her only escape. By the strong sickening smell of his smoker's breath, she knew his face was close—she didn't move. She was hoping he would be content just lying beside her, watching and listening to her sleep.

At the same time she felt his hand on her breast, she felt his wet, nasty lips cover her mouth. Panic flowed through her as she pushed and kicked with all her strength. He fell to the floor. She rolled to the far side of the bed, braced her back against the wall, and positioned her feet and legs in a defensive position.

"You little bitch!"

She felt her bedspread move and heard his hands sliding over her sheet as he searched for her. She could not see him; she assumed he was still on the floor, just below the faint light coming from her window, probably on his knees.

"Where are you?" Then, using the same pleading voice she heard him use earlier with her mother, he said, "Come here, honey. I promise I won't hurt you."

She pulled her thighs tight against her chest and pointed her legs and feet toward his voice; she was ready to strike.

"Come on, sweetie," he pleaded. There was a long pause before he spoke. "I'll come back later."

The light from the window was enough for Angie to see him stand, then move toward her door. She didn't know if he could see her but sensed that he knew she was prepared to kick him if he touched her. The sound of her door opening and closing brought her comfort; he was no longer in her room.

Anger engulfed her when she heard John say to her mother, "She'll get used to it."

She wanted to shout and tell him it would never happen again, but she didn't want to part her lips and taste John's nasty mouth; the smell was bad enough.

She was anxious to wash her mouth and face, but before leaving her room, she waited until there was no sound coming from her mother and John's bedroom. Then, with her mouth closed so tight her jaw hurt, she slowly opened her door and felt her way to the bathroom. She locked the door but did not turn on the light. Not having the memory of seeing herself in the mirror was most important. She washed once, washed twice, then washed again. Even after washing the fourth time, she still felt dirty.

Finally, she realized it would take more than washing to erase the feel and memory of his mouth covering hers. Not only did she feel violated, she felt as if her mother had used her. The disgusting abuse she suffered from John was bad, but knowing her mother had condoned and even suggested that he go to her was worse. She lost control of her emotions and began to sob.

Angie did not try to muffle her crying. She wanted her mother to know how heartbroken she was. But more than anything, she wanted her mother to join her in the bathroom, take her in her arms, and tell her how sorry she was and it would never happen again.

When it was obvious that her mother was not concerned, she returned to her room. She held her father's picture close.

"Don't worry, Dad. He'll never do that again." She pulled the covers over her and her father's picture and began planning her defense. The sun was rising when she finally fell asleep, but her plan was finalized.

Angie was sitting at the kitchen table, drinking a glass of milk. She felt sick and thought a little milk might help settle her stomach. It was Saturday and no school. She hoped to be out of the house before John or her mother woke. The milk was working and she began to feel better, but that changed when she looked up and saw John standing in the doorway. She felt nauseated and couldn't finish her milk.

She stood, turned her back to him, poured what was left of her milk in the sink, and rinsed her glass. The thought of him standing behind her was overwhelming. She began to tremble; her stomach felt as if it were in her throat and ready to explode. She felt awkward standing at the sink, not knowing if he was still standing in the doorway or walking up behind her. Cautiously, she slowly turned to face him. He had entered the room and was sitting at the table.

She watched as he nonchalantly opened a new pack of cigarettes, tapped one out, put it in his mouth, and lit it. Now the small room was filled with smoke, which only added to her discomfort. He was not wearing a shirt, and the smell of stale smoke mixed with several days of perspiration rose from his body. The smell was sickening, even at the sink—she was reminded of the way he smelled the night before. Her throat began to tighten, but she held back the tears. Out of the corner of her eye, she looked in the direction of the door, the door leading outside. She turned and had taken a step toward it when she heard him say "Good morning" as if nothing had happened.

She spun around, looked him in the eyes, and shouted, "If you ever come in my room again, I'll kill you!"

Again, she started for the door but stopped when she saw her mother enter the room. A cigarette dangled from the corner of her mouth, her stringy hair covered one eye, her head was cocked to one side to protect the uncovered eye from the smoke. While pulling out a chair from the table with one hand, she lifted the strap of her dirty nightgown with the other; it had fallen down her arm, exposing a breast.

When Angie saw them smiling at each other, she screamed at John, "I meant what I said! And you better stay out of my room!" Then she directed her anger to her mother, "And I can't believe you encouraged him! I hate you! I hate you both!"

She turned her back to them and bolted for the door, letting it slam behind her. She ran for several blocks, and when she could no longer run, she walked. She had no idea where she was going; she just had to get away.

Not being familiar with the neighborhood and getting uncomfortable, she turned around and began walking back toward John's trailer. Going back and dealing with John and her mother was a chore she preferred to put off for as long as possible.

What am I going to do? Where can I go? I know. I'll go stay in that old shed behind John's trailer.

She cautiously walked through the neighbors' backyards and made it to the shed without being seen. Being alone in the small shed, isolated from the rest of the world, brought her comfort, and for a while, her experience from the night before seemed as if it were a bad dream—she fell asleep wondering what the night would bring.

An engine starting woke her. She looked out one of the cracks. John and her mother were leaving. *Whew! At least now I can go in and use the bathroom.*

After using the bathroom, she searched in her closet for the baseball bat her dad had given her. The bat brought back some great memories, memories of her dad pitching to her, and how, when she made contact, he always complimented her by saying, "Good hit!" Her eyes began to tear and her throat began to tighten. "I wish you were here to protect me, Dad. But you're not. So I guess I'll have to take care of myself."

A car door closed, then another. *They're home!* She hid the baseball bat under the covers and pretended to be asleep. Her door opened and then it closed. She barely opened her eyes, discovered no one in her room, then heard her mother say, "She's in her room."

John began to sweet-talk her mother. They went into their room, and Angie was forced to listen to their disgusting sounds. Again, she placed her pillow over her head, trying to muffle the sounds, and again, it was little help. She wanted to leave her room but didn't want her squeaky door to announce that she was awake.

A few hours later, Angie's door opened a little. Without entering, her mother said they were going for a bucket of chicken. Angie waited until she saw them pull away, then went to the phone and called her grandmother, her mother's mother.

"Hi, Grandma."

"Hi, Angie. How are you doing?"

"Not so good. Can I come live with you?"

"You know I'd love for you to be here with me. I hate the thoughts of you being with your mom and that sorry man, but there's nothing I can do. We both have asked her if you can live with me, and for the life of me, I can't understand why she won't let you."

"Please, Grandma, please come get me. I have to get out of here today."

"By the sound of your voice, it seems really bad."

"It is, Grandma. You can't imagine how bad."

"Is your mom there?"

"No, they went to get something to eat."

"Well, it's too late to come over today. It'd be best if she's sober when we talk, and being this late in the day, I'm sure she's not. Tomorrow is Sunday and I have a full day of church activities planned. So Monday morning, I'll go to your school and talk to whoever can help us. At least after talking with them, I'll have a better idea of what our legal rights are. Then that afternoon, before your mom gets too intoxicated, I'll drop by and talk with her. Hopefully, you'll be able to come home with me. Can you make it till then?"

"I'll try."

"Trust me, Angie. I know it's difficult, and I'll get you out of that mess as soon as I can. We just have to make sure the law is on our side. In the meantime, try to not rock the boat."

"I'll do my best to stay away from them, but in a trailer this small, it won't be easy."

"I know. Do the best you can, and call me if things get too bad."

"I will. Thanks, Grandma."

"I'll see you Monday. I love you, Angie."

"I love you too, Grandma."

At the same time Angie finished talking with her grandmother, she saw John's car pull into the driveway. She ran back to her room and jumped in bed.

Her door opened; it was her mother.

"We know our cigarette smoke bothers you, and you'd refuse to eat with us, so we bought you a two-piece dinner." She placed the bag with the dinner on the foot of the bed and left without saying another word.

Even though her mother had left the room and the door was closed, the foul odor that filled the room was as if she were still there. The rank smell of body odor, that an effort had been made to disguise with cheap perfume, mixed with cigarette smoke and beer had killed Angie's appetite.

Soon, the aroma of chicken dominated. Perhaps it was her hunger that allowed it. She opened the bag, took out the box of chicken, the warm can of cola, and began eating. At first, she picked at the food, but soon, she was eating with both hands. It was like she had not eaten in a week, and before she knew it, it was gone; she wished there had been more. She finished the cola and put the can and the other trash in the bag. When she returned from washing her hands, she locked her door, cuddled up to her baseball bat, and was soon asleep.

Angie was up early. John and her mother had stayed up late. The last time Angie looked at her clock, it was 2:00 a.m. and they were still up. *This is good. They will sleep late, probably until noon.*

While eating her bowl of cereal, she evaluated the condition of the kitchen: *What a filthy rat hole. How can anyone live like this? I'm going to leave, even if Grandma can't get me out. I don't know what I'll do or where I'll go, but I'm leaving. And I'm not going to stay cooped up in my room again today. I'll go for a walk and think about it.*

It seemed that walking brought her comfort and relieved her tension. After walking for several hours, she was thinking clearer. Except for her grandmother, Angie had no other family to confide in or go to for assistance. Her father's parents died several years before his accident. He had no brothers or sisters.

If Grandma doesn't come get me, I'll talk with the guidance counselor. There's one thing I know for sure, I won't stay in that trailer more than one more night. If Grandma or the counselor can't help me, I'll go to the police. And if none of them will help, I'll hit the streets. I might as well go home and start packing. I hope they're still sleeping.

Angie

Angie managed to have her few clothes packed and ready to go without waking them. She hid the bags containing her meager belongings under her bed, took a cola from the refrigerator, put two pieces of chicken in a plastic bag, and left—fortunately, her mother or John had remembered to put the chicken in the refrigerator before going to bed.

It was almost noon when she found herself back in the security of the dark old shed. Thinking that she should not let the lunch she packed get warm, she ate the chicken and drank the cola, then after a short nap, went for another walk.

When she returned, it was getting dark. John and her mother were sitting at the table. John was not wearing a shirt, and as usual, the room was filled with smoke. When Angie saw the anger on her mother's face and in her eyes, she knew she was in trouble.

"Where have you been?" her mother shouted.

"I just took a little walk."

"A little walk, my ass. You've been gone for hours!"

"I'm sorry. I didn't realize it was this late. I won't do it again."

"You damn right you won't do it again! You're grounded for two weeks! And I better not catch you out of this house!"

Angie wanted to say, "Don't you mean 'house-trailer,'" but instead, she chose to be tactful. "I'm sorry. I'm not feeling well and the smoke is burning my eyes. So if you don't mind, I'll take a shower and go to bed."

"You little baby. 'The smoke is burning my eyes.'"

"Don't use all the hot water," John demanded.

Like he's actually going to take a shower.

After her shower, she locked her door, got her baseball bat from under the bed, then pulled the sheet over her and the bat. She wasn't sleepy but dozed off while thinking how that night was going to be the last with her mother and, especially, John.

CHAPTER 2

Angie looked at the clock, 12:30. Something had awakened her. She sat up and listened. The room was quiet, so quiet she could hear herself breathe. She looked toward the door, where she thought the sound had come from, then reached for her baseball bat. She heard it again. *He's trying to unlock my door!*

"Don't come in here!" she screamed.

The sound continued.

Holding her bat, she jumped out of bed. The room was dark as pitch; she had to feel her way to where she planned to be if this happened. *It will be best if the light is off. That way, if he sees the bat, and being larger than me, he could take it, leaving me defenseless.*

She held the bat as if she were going to hit a home run—just like her father taught her. "I'm warning you! I have a bat, and I'm not afraid to use it!" She waited and listened as he struggled with the lock. *What if it's Mom? I'll have to wait and be sure. Oh, God. Can I do this?* She thought back to the last time he was in her room. *Yes. I can do this. And I warned him.* Her heart was pounding, her knees were weak, and her legs were trembling, but she held her stance. *Please let it be Mom. I don't want to do this.*

The sound of her door unlocking, then the familiar squeak as it began to open, caused her heart to pound even harder. She flexed her hands around the bat until comfortable, then tightened her grip, an image began coming in. She had to wait. *Oh, please, let it be Mom.*

"Hi, honey. Look what I have for you, again."

"I don't think so!"

She aimed for his head and swung with all her strength, hitting him in the face.

"Good hit, Angie!" she heard her father say.

The force of the blow knocked him out of her room, and by the direction of his moans, she knew he was lying on the floor. When Angie's shaking hand finally found the light switch and turned it on, she almost passed out. The shock of seeing his naked body stretched out before her, the blood seeping between the fingers of the hand that covered his mouth and the other bloody hand pounding the floor was almost more than she could handle. She felt sick, and to support her weak, trembling legs from buckling, she leaned against her door.

As she watched him twist with pain and listened to his moans, she almost felt sorry for him. Her pity quickly changed to anger when her mother entered the room.

"What the fuck have you done?" she screamed. "Get me a towel!"

"Get your own towel."

"Why, you disrespectful bitch! Give me that bat!"

Angie raised the bat. "Stay away from me! I warned him—now I'm warning you."

Her mother got a towel from the bathroom and placed in over John's mouth. Then, to cover her naked body, she went back into her bedroom and put on a robe. She returned with John's pants. Angie watched without offering to help as her mother struggled to hold the towel on John's mouth while at the same time assist him with his pants.

"Thanks for all your help!" her mother said sarcastically as she helped John to his feet. "I'm taking him to the hospital."

Still clutching her bat, Angie followed them to the door.

While holding the door open for John, her mother turned back to Angie.

"I'll take care of you when I return," she threatened.

"I can hardly wait to hear how you explain what happened."

As soon as her mother was out of the driveway, she went to the phone. "Grandma, a terrible thing has happened, you have to come get me."

"Now?"

"Yes. Please, now."

"Okay. I'll be right there. You can tell me what's going on when I get there."

Angie dressed quickly. She wanted to be ready to leave when her grandmother arrived. She placed the bags she had packed earlier and the rest of her things by the kitchen door. The kitchen door was used as the main entrance.

Each time she went into her room, she had to step over John's blood. She made no attempt to clean it and wasn't going to. That was something she wanted her mother to do. She washed the blood off the bat and put it with the rest of her stuff.

As soon as her grandmother entered the kitchen, she made a face as if she smelled something bad. "My god. I had no idea you were living in this much filth. You poor child. What happened?"

"You better sit down," Angie said as she pulled a chair from under the table.

Without leaving anything out, Angie told her everything that had occurred, including the first night he came into her room. Her grandmother's face expressed both shock and grief as Angie told her the gory details. When Angie finished, her grandmother put both elbows on the table, placed her face in her hands, and wept. Her face moved from side to side in disbelief.

Her grandmother slowly lifted her face from her hands and looked up at Angie. Angie knelt beside her and melted into her open arms. They held each other close, and Angie began to cry, which caused her grandmother to cry even more. Their cheeks were pressed together, their faces wet with tears.

"You poor baby," her grandmother said when she gained control of her emotions. "I'm so sorry. I should've checked on you days ago or at least when you called. If I had, none of this would've happened. I'm so sorry."

"That's okay. You did the best you could. Maybe, when I called, I should've explained in more detail. If only he hadn't chosen tonight to return to my room. I would've been gone tomorrow."

"I'm getting sick. Let's get your stuff and get out of here."

"My things are right here."

"Is this all you have?"

"This is it."

"Is this the bat you hit him with?"

"Yep. That's my weapon."

"Wow. I bet that hurt."

Her grandmother wrote a note, and they left.

By the time they arrived at her grandmother's house, it was two o'clock. Soon after unloading the car, Angie took a shower and went to bed. Her grandmother suggested they wait until morning before they unpack and get organized.

Angie tried but couldn't sleep. When she closed her eyes, she returned to her small bedroom in John's trailer. She would see her door opening, hear the bat, see his nude body twitching with pain, and the blood. Blood everywhere: on his hands, on his face, in his hair, on the floor, on her bat. She had to open her eyes to stop the images, but the relief was only temporary. Her eyes were too tired to stay open, and when they closed, the dreams returned. In one of her dreams, her mother was coming toward her with bloody hands and smiling as she tried to rub them in Angie's face.

When her grandmother turned on the light, Angie was sitting up in bed, screaming, with her arms flailing the air.

"Angie, honey! Wake up! Wake up! It's just a dream."

Angie opened her eyes as her grandmother was taking her in her arms. "Oh, Grandma. I'm so afraid. I think I hit him too hard. I didn't mean to, but I was so scared. I don't want him to die."

"He's not going to die. I'm sure you didn't hit him that hard."

"Yes, I did. I hit him really hard. Maybe I should've turned on the light and threatened him."

"No, Angie, you did the right thing. If the light was on, you probably would've lost your nerve, or if you did swing at him, he could've defended himself, and that would've only made him angry. There's no telling what he would've done to you if he lost what little control he had. Think of it this way: he'll heal. He may have some scars, but he'll heal. If he had his way with you, it could be that you would never heal. Better him than you.

"Not only would you have to suffer with the emotional scars from what he did to you, your mother would defend him, causing the authorities to doubt you. Knowing that he and your mother got away with it would be difficult to live with. You did say your mother encouraged him?"

"Yes, she did."

"That bothers me."

"Me too."

"Let's try to not think about it and get some sleep."

"Will you sleep with me?"

"Sure."

Angie's grandmother put one arm around her and cuddled close to her back. Angie not only felt the warmth of her grandmother, she felt her love.

"Good night, Grandma."

"Good night, Angie."

CHAPTER 3

Before Angie and her grandmother put Angie's clothes and other belongings away, they fixed a large breakfast. And by the sounds of pleasure Angie made, it was obvious to her grandmother that it had been a while since she had eaten a decent breakfast.

"Thanks, Grandma, this is the best breakfast I've ever had."

"You mean it's the best breakfast you can remember having."

"You're probably right. Dad always cooked breakfast. He made the best pancakes, and his omelets were super. You know, not once do I remember Mom cooking breakfast."

"I don't doubt it."

"Was she always like that?" Angie asked.

"Yes, from the time she was a little girl."

"It's hard for me to imagine her being that way, especially being raised by a mother as clean and neat as you."

"She was a difficult child. I always looked forward to the day she would be big enough and old enough to join me in the kitchen. I didn't really need her help, I just wanted to teach her and answer her questions, like my mother did me. I thought cooking together was going to be a bonding experience, and the kitchen would be our special place, a place where we could be buddies. But that never happened. If she made a mistake or something she was fixing didn't turn out right, she'd throw it in the sink and stomp out of the kitchen. Instead of criticizing or complaining, I tried to encourage her to try again, but she wouldn't. She had no patience, and I found it impossible to work with her—and not only in the kitchen.

"No matter how much I pleaded with her to clean her room, she never did, especially when she became a teenager. And the one time I cleaned it, when she was a teen, she cursed me and told me to never go in her room again. When I forced her to help with the housework, she made it more of a mess than before she started and usually broke something. I stopped asking when I got tired of seeing bleach stains on my rugs and carpet, my furniture scratched, and my most cherished mementos broken or missing. I'm sure she did it on purpose.

"Every stage of life was worse than the one before, and by the time she was in her late teens, she was impossible. She skipped school, stayed out late, started smoking, and acted as if your granddad and I weren't even alive. We grounded her and confined her to her room, but that never worked. When her trashy boyfriends drove up and beeped their horn, she brazenly defied us and left with them. We tried everything. We even tried counseling with the state juvenile authorities. All they did was blame your granddad and me for our daughter's problems. After a few sessions with them, we felt we had to be the worst parents alive. They chose to believe her lies instead of us.

"We finally received some comfort from the counselor at our church. He told us that she was the problem, not us. And she would always be a problem for whomever she's with. He also said we had set a good example, and she was old enough to know right from wrong. His advice was 'Tough love is the only way you can help her. You've done all you can. Now you need to separate yourself from her and go on with your lives. If you don't, she'll control and worry you into an early grave.' He went on to say, 'If she burns her behind, she'll have to sit on the blister. So remember, she's responsible for her actions, and she'll have to suffer the consequences.'

"Your mother was sixteen when we talked with the counselor. I believed what he said to be true, but your granddad didn't. I acted as if I didn't know she existed. Oh sure, I cooked for her, washed her clothes, bought her clothes, and cleaned up after her, but that was about all. Your granddad wouldn't give up. He'd ask about her grades and get a smart answer in return. He tried to instruct her on how to improve her life. She told him she knew what she was doing and didn't appreciate him butting into her business. He tried so hard to show his love and get close to her. The counselor was right: his efforts only caused him grief.

"It's my opinion the grief she caused your granddad was what brought about his heart attack and death. I'll never forgive her for that. He was only forty-five."

She was silent for a moment. "The best thing that happened to your mother was she got pregnant with you, and your father married her."

"You mean Dad and Mom had to get married?"

"You didn't know?"

"No, I didn't. But I always suspected they did."

"I'm sorry. For some reason, I thought you knew."

"That's okay, Grandma. I can handle knowing. It sounds like Mom knew several men. How did she know I was Dad's?"

"I don't know the details. I only know your father knew, and he was determined to do the right thing. And it doesn't take a genius to know he was right. You look and act just like him."

"I'm glad you told me about Mom. I have always known she was mean, but I thought the stress of Dad's death was the reason she started drinking, which caused her to be even more hateful."

"No, Angie. I hate to say it, but your mother was born bad. And the sooner you realize there's nothing you can change, the better off you'll be. I know this sounds cruel, but if you are sympathetic and try to help, you'll find that you are the only one suffering. Your granddad, your father, and I gave her every opportunity imaginable to change. But she resented our efforts and chose to be what she is. As the counselor predicted: she burned her behind, and now she has to sit on the blister."

While helping Angie unpack, her grandmother couldn't help but notice the bad condition of her clothes. And there were no bras.

"I have to do some shopping today, so if you like, you can come with me and we'll pick up a few things for you."

She tried to make Angie feel comfortable about going shopping without giving her a complex about the condition of her clothes.

"Shouldn't you be at work?"

"Yes, and you should be in school. But today, we have more important things to worry about. Like getting you settled into your new home and finding out what school you'll be attending. I called work and told them I'd be taking a couple days off."

Angie was looking forward to having some new clothes and especially anxious to finally own some bras, but she didn't want her grandmother to feel obligated to buy them. "I really appreciate you letting me live with you, Grandma, but I don't want you to spend your money on me. I'll find a way."

"Now, Angie. I don't want you to worry about me buying you things. I know I don't have to, but I want to. And I want you to feel comfortable when I do. So pamper your old grandma and let me treat you like you're my daughter. At least I know you'll appreciate it more than your mother did."

"There's one thing you can be sure of, I will appreciate what you do for me. And you're not old."

"Going on fifty-five."

"That's not old. And you sure don't look it."

"Thanks, Angie."

"Mom gets a check for me each month from Social Security. Can you get it?"

"That's right. I didn't think of that. She won't agree to it, but I'm sure we can convince her."

Their first stop was school. Angie would be going to the same school but taking a different bus. The rest of the day was spent shopping for Angie.

Soon after arriving home and while unloading her grandmother's car, Angie's mother pulled in behind them.

Angie became concerned when her mother began walking toward them; she moved closer to her grandmother. There had been many times when Angie had witnessed those tight wrinkled lips, the rage in her eyes, and the clenched teeth that caused the muscles in her jaws to protrude and flex.

"I see you're already buying her things and trying to turn her against me! Well, it won't work! You can take all this stuff back! She's coming home with me!"

Angie was nervous and scared. Her grandmother was angry but in control.

"I don't think so," her grandmother said.

"What do you mean! She's my daughter, and she'll go where I tell her!" She glared at Angie and pointed to her car. "Get in that car!"

Angie's grandmother put her arm around Angie and held her close. "She's not going anywhere."

"Do you know what she did to my husband?"

"From what Angie tells me he tried to do to her, I hope she did a lot."

"She knocked out all his front teeth, top and bottom. His lips are full of stitches and will never be right. That's what she did."

"Way to go, Angie!" her grandmother said as she tightened her arm around her.

Angie looked up at her grandmother. "I warned him."

"My own mother against me," Angie's mother shouted. "I might've known I'd get no sympathy from you."

"You got that right."

"I'm going to the law! I'll let them come get her!"

"I think that's a good idea. Then Angie and I can file charges against you and your obnoxious husband for child abuse. So why don't you just traipse your sorry ass over to the Sheriff's Department. I can hardly wait to see a deputy pull in my driveway.

"Angie warned your husband, but he didn't listen. Now I'm warning you, and you better listen. If I see you on my property again, I'll have you and your no-account husband arrested. Unfortunately for Angie, I ignored you and what you did with your life, but now that your life is affecting Angie's, I won't ignore you any longer. I regret that I didn't get involved sooner. If I had, Angie wouldn't have had to endure the abuse she did, and your husband would still have his teeth.

"For Angie's sake, I wish I could change what happened, but I can't. But there's one thing I'm sure of: you or your disgusting husband will never hurt her again. And you better hope I don't change my mind about reporting you. And another thing, I want Angie's Social Security check forwarded to her. So if you don't want to get in serious trouble, I suggest you stay away from us and forward her check. Now, get in that car and leave before I call the sheriff."

Angie and her grandmother turned their backs to her and returned to taking their packages from the car. They heard her car back out of the driveway, then heard the engine rev and the tires squeal as she roared away. Her grandmother looked at the smoke from the tires, shook her head, and said, "Just like when she was a teenager."

CHAPTER 4

For the first time since her father's death, Angie enjoyed going to school. Finally, she was wearing bras and no longer felt ashamed of her clothes. Her grandmother cut and shaped her long straggly hair into a short, casual style that was much easier to manage. With her grandmother's help, she became a very attractive thirteen-year-old. Unfortunately, the image the other students had of her was still the same, especially the girls. They still remembered her as a Raggedy Ann and continued to distance themselves.

Angie realized that the pretentious, upper-class girls, or at least those who presumed to be, had no desire to accept her. They had their little conceited groups and thought of themselves as better than everyone else. To her, being accepted by them, or even being recognized as a person of equal significance, was not of any importance. Unlike most girls, she didn't require the constant companionship of others.

Because she chose to not socialize, most of the other students thought of her as snobbish. Having friends was not that important; she was content just being alone or with her grandmother.

Three weeks after Angie moved in with her grandmother, they received their first Social Security check. Now she could stop worrying about being a burden to her grandmother. The check came to her mother; she had endorsed it and mailed it to them. Evidently, Angie's mother had paid attention to what her grandmother said would happen if she didn't.

Angie and her grandmother became very close and spent as much time together as possible. They went shopping and to movies, cleaned the house, did yard work, and were involved with many other activities. But the one thing Angie liked doing most was cooking, and her grandmother enjoyed teaching just as much as Angie liked learning. Going to church was the only activity she did not enjoy.

She was not familiar with church procedures and rituals and wasn't sure how to conduct herself. Her mother and father were not religious and never went; attending church was something new to her. Most of the time, she felt that her grandmother and she were the only ones listening to the service. The others were too busy admiring themselves or talking about how someone else looked. The majority of the congregation was there, not to listen, but rather to be seen and heard.

She would have preferred to stay home, but her grandmother's belief was strong, and going to church gave her spiritual comfort. It brought her grandmother even more comfort knowing Angie was with her, and she was not going to let her grandmother down.

Angie woke to find her room bright with light. She looked at the clock by her bed, 2:00 a.m. When she realized the light was coming from outside, she became concerned. It had been six weeks since she last saw her mother.

"Grandma!" she shouted. "Someone's here!"

"Can you see who it is?"

"No. Their lights are too bright."

"Let's check it out."

They arrived at the door at the same time as the deputy. Angie's grandmother knew the deputy and also knew something had happened.

"Hi, Dick. What's wrong?"

"I have some bad news. Your daughter and her husband's mobile home caught fire, and they didn't survive."

"They're dead?"

"I'm sorry."

Angie and her grandmother put their arms around each other and wept. Even though they had not been close to Angie's mother, it was sad to know she was gone. When her grandmother regained enough composure to talk, she thanked the deputy for letting them know.

They stayed up the rest of the night discussing the arrangements. By morning, they had agreed to not get their church involved or have a large funeral. They didn't know what John's family wanted.

It was early that morning when John's sister called. It did not take long for Angie's grandmother to realize that John's family wanted to take charge of the arrangements and have a large double funeral at their church.

"Do whatever you want," she told his sister, "but don't expect Angie or me to help or get involved."

"I can't believe how unconcerned you seem to be!"

"Believe it!" Angie's grandmother said, then hung up the phone.

As John's family wanted, it was a large funeral. Angie and her grandmother attended, but instead of sitting up front in the family section, they chose an area in the back, close to the door. It was a small church, and even though they were sitting as far from John's family as possible, they were still close enough to see and hear their exaggerated crying and wailing and their dramatic behavior. Some would fall to the floor as they wept; others helped them to their feet, only to see them fall again.

Angie whispered to her grandmother, "You'd think he was a really nice guy."

"I know. It's ridiculous, isn't it?"

After a few minutes into the service, Angie put her head on her grandmother's shoulder and began to cry. She wasn't grieving for her mother; she wasn't even thinking about her. She had thought back to her father's death and funeral. "I miss Dad so much, Grandma."

Her grandmother put her arm around her and pulled her close. "I know you do. And I understand."

"I wish I could control my tears," Angie said while she and her grandmother were on their way home. "But ever since Dad's death, I have become a real crybaby. I cry when I'm sad. I cry when I'm happy. I cry while holding a new baby, a puppy, or a kitten. I even cry when I see a dead animal beside the road. There's times I'm the only one with tears in their eyes when the teacher or a student reads a sad story or a story that expresses a lot of love and has an excellent ending. I don't remember being this way while Dad was alive. I guess his death and funeral turned on my tears, and I can't seem to turn them off. I try, but I just can't hide my emotions."

Her grandmother glanced toward her, then back to the road. "No, Angie. Your father's death isn't the reason, it's in your genes. Your Dad was the most emotional person I have ever known. I was with him the day you were born, and when the nurse placed you in his arms, he couldn't say a word. His chin trembled and his eyes filled with tears as he admired you for the first time. When he took you into your mother's room and she saw that he had been crying, she made fun of him and accused him of being a wimp. To my knowledge, he never allowed her to see his tears again.

"I went with you and your father to most of your school plays and sporting events, your mother never went. His eyes would fill with tears as he watched and listened to you perform on stage. He did the same when you did well in sports and when you didn't. I'm sure there were times when he wished he could've expressed himself without his throat tightening to where he couldn't speak. But fortunately, his lack of control never seemed to concern him when we were together. He loved me as if I were his mother, and I loved him as if he were my son.

"Your dad had very few friends, you were his life, and I felt honored to have been included in his and your activities."

"Occasionally, I saw that Dad's eyes were red, but I didn't know he had to struggle to maintain his composure. But I do remember this one time he had to wipe his eyes while signing my report card."

"Would you remember him signing your report card if you hadn't seen his tears?"

"Probably not."

"Doesn't that tell you something?"

"That I should never be ashamed or embarrassed when I express my emotions and show my true feelings?"

"Right! So the next time you're trying to hold back your tears, remember the report card."

"I will. Thanks, Grandma."

Even though Angie and her grandmother were close and joined in many activities, she was still very lonely. Most of their activities were related to church projects, such as baking for bake sales, then selling what they baked, entertaining people in nursing homes, and visiting church members at local hospitals, none of which were of any interest to a thirteen-year-old. After six months of being patient and doing whatever her grandmother wanted, she became bored.

Her grandmother never watched anything but religious programs on TV and only listened to gospel music. It was difficult for Angie to keep up with the news or comment on a popular TV program with her classmates. So instead of asking her grandmother for a TV for her room, she began babysitting for several families from church. For her fourteenth birthday, her grandmother added enough money to what she had saved to buy a small TV for her bedroom. Two months later, she saved enough for a small stereo.

Angie's grandmother had never tried to force her to watch or listen to what she preferred, and Angie didn't want to be inconsiderate and subject her grandmother to something she wasn't comfortable with. By her having her own TV and stereo, they could entertain themselves without disturbing the other.

⤳

Angie continued to be a loner and not be part of any particular group of kids. She was friendly with all but had few friends; she preferred her privacy. To her, having good grades was most important, and she did. Not only was she a straight A student, she excelled in athletics, which had the coaches competing; each tried to encourage her to join their team.

She was an excellent swimmer and diver, and her long shapely legs helped make her exceptionally good at running and jumping. Because of this, the swimming and track coaches were always talking to her, but even though she was not tall (5'6"), the basketball coach was the most persistent. What she lacked in height, she made up in quickness. He told her that he could almost guarantee a scholarship.

She wanted a scholarship, but in academics, not sports, and to achieve her goal, she had to keep up her grades. Getting the required rest, if involved with sports, would only interfere with her studying. She would have to start going to bed earlier and give up her babysitting jobs; she could not afford that. Babysitting also made it convenient to study and do her homework while the children slept.

⤳

During the summer, before starting the eleventh grade, Angie turned sixteen. Soon after school started, she finished the driver's education class and received her driver's license. She was allowed to use her grandmother's car whenever she wanted; she welcomed her new freedom and never abused her privilege. Having the use of a car made it much easier to babysit. She no longer had to depend on her grandmother or the people she babysat for to provide her transportation. It gave her a feeling of independence.

Angie

Angie had looked forward to being sixteen. Her grandmother had asked her to wait until she was sixteen before dating. Several boys in her class had asked her for a date when she was fourteen and fifteen, but she politely refused. But now that she was sixteen, no one asked, and she couldn't understand why. During the last two years, she had matured much more than the boys she grew up with; now they seemed shy, less assertive, and insecure. They weren't up to the challenge.

Angie was not conceited but was very much aware of her good looks and her trim, well-proportioned figure. She always dressed casually, but with good taste, and never looked tacky or cheap. She chose her clothes to accent her figure, and with her thin waist, broad shoulders, shapely hips and behind, that was not difficult. Her grandmother cut her hair as good as any beautician, and they had perfected her hairstyle. It was short and casual, making her long neck look even longer. Her large smile showed her beautiful, well-kept, sparkling white teeth. And when she smiled, her whole face smiled, especially her dark brown eyes. Her grandmother had always told her she was beautiful, and now she was starting to believe her. Her grandmother also said the reason the boys were reluctant to ask her out was because they felt intimidated.

Angie and her grandmother spent Christmas morning alone, but they were not lonely. Angie was impressed with how much her grandmother enjoyed opening her presents. And just like the three Christmases before, she acted more like a child than Angie. A few days earlier, a friend at church had introduced Angie's grandmother to a man about her age whose wife had died a few months earlier. His name was Wayne. When she discovered he was going to be alone for Christmas, she invited him to dinner. He had accepted her invitation and would arrive later that evening. Angie and her grandmother looked forward to having someone to cook for. This was the first Christmas that someone had joined them for dinner, and they had prepared a large meal.

Their timing was perfect: The table was set and dinner was ready when Wayne arrived. After dinner and thinking that her grandmother would like to get to know Wayne, Angie volunteered to pick up the dishes and clean the kitchen. When the kitchen was clean, she made coffee and prepared the dessert, apple pie and ice cream. She served the dessert and coffee in the living room, then joined them.

"This pie is excellent. Did you ladies bake it?"

"Grandma did."

"You are a good cook, Grandma."

They laughed, and she thanked him.

"Angie, do you mind if I ask your age?"

"No, not at all. I'm sixteen."

"You look older than sixteen. What grade are you in?"

"I'm a junior."

"Would you be interested in meeting my grandson?"

"I'm not sure. How old is he?"

"He's seventeen. He's a senior at Bayshore High. Maybe you know him? Bob Davis?"

"No. I don't know him. I attend Manatee High."

"How about you and your grandmother joining Bob and me at my house this Saturday for a cookout? That way, you can meet him. Then you and Bob can take it from there. What do you think?"

"Sounds like a good idea to me. What do you think, Grandma?"

"Sounds good to me."

"I'll start cooking about six o'clock, so come early, about two or three. Will that work for you?"

"That'll work for me. How about you, Grandma?"

"Fine. Looking forward to it."

"I guess you're wondering," Wayne said, "if I have a grandson, why am I not having Christmas dinner with his parents?"

Angie's grandmother gave him a puzzled look. "Yes, it does seem a little strange."

"Bob's mother, my son's wife, and I have a bad personality conflict, so we keep our distance. I don't get to spend as much time with my son and grandson as I'd like, but it's best if I'm not around her. They understand."

Angie

Bob arrived soon after Angie and her grandmother. After introducing them, Wayne asked Angie's grandmother if he could fix her a drink.

"I'm drinking bourbon, but I have about anything. I make a great margarita. Can I mix you one?"

"No, thank you."

"How about a glass of wine?"

"No, thank you. I don't drink."

"Not at all?"

"Not at all."

Angie was certain her grandmother had no idea that a man who attended her church would drink. It was obvious, especially since she was a teetotaler, that she was uncomfortable but mostly disappointed.

Bob was everything Angie had hoped he would be: tall, good-looking, outgoing, courteous, and witty. But there was something about him she was not comfortable with. She could not figure out why she was reluctant to warm to his obvious attempts to woo her. He seemed a little too anxious.

Wayne prepared an excellent meal. The steaks were cooked to perfection, and the rest of the meal expressed his desire to please. Both Angie and her grandmother were impressed with Wayne's ability to drink without getting intoxicated. They had never been around someone who drank and still functioned. Most of the people they had been exposed to that drank, drank to get drunk. Angie could tell that his ability to hold his liquor didn't impress her grandmother enough to accept the fact that he was an excellent person in spite of his drinking.

Bob asked Angie if she'd like to take a ride to the beach. It seemed like a good idea to her; by being alone they could get to know each other better, but her grandmother's expression was not encouraging.

"I'd love to," she said, "but I think we should be getting home." She saw the relief in her grandmother's eyes. "Maybe another day?"

"Do you have plans for tomorrow?"

"Not yet."

"How about tomorrow?"

"Tomorrow will be fine."

"I'll call you in the morning."

Angie and her grandmother thanked Wayne for a wonderful dinner and evening. Wayne said he would call, but Angie knew that he and her grandmother had not hit it off too well, and he would not be calling.

Bob's aggressive behavior convinced Angie that he felt she was easy. She may not have dated before, but she wasn't naive. Their first night together and after only three kisses, he had tried to fondle her breast. She pushed him away and said she was not ready for that, and if he didn't stop, he could take her home. He stopped for the night. The next night, he tried again but with more respect and caution. He was quick to stop when she resisted.

During the last week of the Christmas vacation, Angie and Bob spent as much time together as possible. The nights she didn't have to babysit, they went to a movie or out to dinner, and sometimes, they drove to the beach to watch the sunset. The days were spent swimming at the beach or driving around talking. One day, Bob borrowed his grandfather's boat, and they went fishing and skiing. By the time they returned to school, they knew each other quite well, and Angie was getting over her skepticism.

She found that her thoughts were always about Bob and how much she cared for him. When she wasn't with him, she could hardly wait until their next date. It seemed that he was the only thing on her mind, which made it difficult to study and do homework.

After several weeks of dating, he told her he loved her. She was quick to respond, "I love you too." She wasn't sure if she did, but at the time, it seemed like the right thing to say. There had been many nights she couldn't sleep and lay awake longing to be in his arms and feel his passionate kisses as his hands gently caressed familiar areas and cautiously searched for new ones. *Maybe I do love him, or am I confusing lust with love. I don't think so. I hope he's not.*

Because of her feelings and after hearing him say he loved her, she found it difficult to resist his desire to touch and explore. She continued to resist his advances, but not with the same intensity as before. She wasn't being a tease; she was scared and being cautious. She felt guilty each time she found herself letting him advance a little, and it took several dates before she was comfortable enough to let him continue. Even though she enjoyed the feel of him touching and caressing those sensitive parts of her body, she was determined to not allow him to have his way with her.

Angie and Bob were with each other at least once a week and sometimes twice. He continually told her he loved her and wanted to be with her the rest of his life. He also told her he had never had sex and she would be his first and only. But only when she was ready.

Angie felt certain he knew she was a virgin and was surprised when he told her he had never had sex. Even though he had lied to her before, she wanted to believe him but wasn't sure. After more than three months of dating, they had experienced everything but intercourse. She desired to go all the way as much as Bob but was going to wait until she was convinced of his sincerity. There was no question about her feelings for him—they were strong, and when she told him it came from her heart, she meant it.

It was a week before Easter when Angie asked Bob to accompany her and her grandmother to church on Easter Sunday. To her surprise, he said he would love to. Angie and her grandmother had asked him many times before to go to church with them, but he always refused. He told them he was uncomfortable on the few occasions he had attended. It was obvious to Angie that he had rather not go and was going just to please her. *He must really love me.*

∽

Angie could tell that Bob was uncomfortable in church, especially when those who had not attended in over a year were asked to stand. He wasn't going to, but her grandmother insisted and was making a scene while trying to encourage him. With much reluctance and embarrassment, he stood. He was the only one standing. Her grandmother was proud to be the only member who brought someone who qualified. Angie felt sorry for him.

As he was driving them home, Angie told him she realized it was a trying experience and she appreciated him going. Her grandmother also thanked him and invited him to dinner.

Before, during, and after dinner, Angie admired how comfortable her grandmother was with Bob. It seemed that going to church had made him more credible; now, he was a person she was willing to accept.

∽

Later that evening, Angie and Bob drove to their favorite parking spot at the beach and, as usual, began to pet. Somehow, she felt closer to him—maybe it was because he went to church or maybe it was because he looked more handsome than usual or maybe it was the respect he had shown her grandmother. Whatever the reason, she was anxious to express her affection.

The thought of going all the way had been on her mind for several hours, and she was so nervous she could hardly swallow. When the petting and fondling progressed to the point she normally began resisting, she allowed him to continue. Then, to his disbelief, she unbuckled her belt and unzipped her jeans. She felt him trembling as he helped her remove her jeans and underwear. While he was removing his shirt and pants, she lifted her T-shirt and bra over her breasts; earlier, when they began petting, he had unhooked her bra.

She was worried and scared but felt a little more comfortable when she knew he was going to be using the protection he took from his glove compartment. *I guess he wanted to be prepared, just in case.*

He came to her, and their passionate kisses expressed their desire.

CHAPTER 5

For the next three weeks, Bob called almost every night, and they had sex as often as possible. They had sex in his car, in the sand on the beach, and on his grandfather's boat. The fourth week he called less and didn't seem to have as much desire to be with her as before. The fifth week was even less. Angie was becoming concerned. When she asked if she had said or done something to upset him, he told her no, he had been busy helping his grandfather with some remodeling.

At the beginning of the sixth week, Angie's grandmother answered the phone.

"It's for you. It's a girl."

"Hello."

"Is this the Angela Blake that goes to Manatee High?"

"Yes."

"My name is Ruby Winston, and I attend Bayshore High. I think we've been dating the same guy."

"You must be mistaken."

"Does your boyfriend own a blue Chevy and is a senior at Bayshore?"

"Yes, but he doesn't have another girlfriend."

"Is his name Bob Davis?"

"Yes."

"I hate to tell you this, but that sorry bastard has been dating both of us."

"I don't believe you."

"I'm sure you don't. I didn't want to believe it either when I found out. I overheard him telling one of his friends how he had gotten another virgin. He told his friend her name was Angie, and she was in the eleventh grade at Manatee High. I didn't want to believe what I heard, so I asked one of my friends at Manatee to check. She did and discovered that you are in the eleventh grade. I still refused to believe he was cheating, so about two weeks ago, I followed him to our favorite place to park."

"At the beach?"

"Yes. At the beach. I thought I was going to die. You can't imagine how much I loved him."

"Yes, I can." Angie didn't want to listen to what Ruby was saying or believe her, but she was starting to realize that what she said was true.

"And guess what else he's doing?"

"What?"

"About two weeks ago, he started dating a fourteen-year-old ninth grader."

"That's about when he started seeing me less. How long have you been dating him?" Angie asked.

"Let's see. It was two months before Christmas. How long have you been seeing him?"

"Since a few days after Christmas."

"That slime ball!" Ruby shouted. "He told me he was busy helping his grandfather, and all the time, he was busy putting the make on you!"

"For the last couple weeks, he's been telling me that he's helping his grandfather with some remodeling."

"Don't believe him."

"Can I call you back? I'm so upset I can hardly think."

Ruby gave Angie her phone number, then said, "I understand. I've had more time than you to get over the shock. Call me when you feel up to it."

Her grandmother could tell by the conversation that something was wrong.

"Is there a problem?"

"I'm afraid so. Ruby, the girl on the phone, told me that Bob is cheating on me. She said for the last several months, she has also been going with him."

"I don't believe her. Didn't you say he told you he was helping Wayne and that's why he couldn't see you?"

"Yes, he did."

"Well, that'll be easy to confirm. Just call Wayne and ask him."

"That's a good idea. What's his number?"

Angie was so nervous she could hardly dial his number.

"Hi, Wayne. This is Angie."

"Hi, Angie. How are you?"

"I'm fine. I'm looking for Bob and thought he might be there."

"No. He's not here. I haven't seen him today."

"How's the remodeling going?"

"What remodeling?"

"I thought Bob said you were doing some remodeling."

"I put in some new storage cabinets in the garage, but that was several months ago."

"I guess I'm confused. I thought he said he was helping you."

"You must be kidding. Bob is a nice guy, but he's also lazy and non-mechanical, and the last thing I'd do is ask him to help me. He can screw up an anvil with a rubber mallet. I hate to say that about my own grandson, but it's true. I don't think I'll see him today, but if I do, would you like me to ask him to give you a call?"

"That's okay. I'll catch him later. It was good talking with you."

Her grandmother knew that Wayne had told Angie what she didn't want to hear. Bob had always been kind to her and treated her with respect, and now she realized that, just like Angie, she had been conned.

"I would've never thought he would do something like that. You just never know."

"I'm finding that out. I'll never trust another man!"

"Now, Angie. Don't compare all men to Bob. There's good and bad in all—men and women. Always remember what fine men your dad and granddad were, and there's a lot more like them. They're just harder to find. The best you can hope for is you won't get hurt while searching for one. Just remember to always trust your instincts."

"That's where I went wrong with Bob. I should've gone with my first instinct. But I was so anxious for companionship that I overlooked his lies and the bad vibes I was feeling. In the beginning, I sensed he was not being honest with me, and his odd personality was not what I would've preferred. But I figured it would all work out in time."

"When I was about your age, my mother told me something. And the older I get, the more I realize how right she was. She said, 'If the man you're with has a habit that bothers you or his personality is difficult to accept or his beliefs are different from yours or he does anything that annoys you, don't stick your head in the sand and think it'll get better—it won't. It can be something simple, like how he smacks when he eats, parts his hair, rolls his eyes, gossips, or dresses. Whatever it is that irritates you in the beginning of a relationship will only get worse.' She also said, 'If you think you can change your way of thinking and after you're married those things that concern you will go away—you're wrong. When your love is new and hot, you're blind to all but what you want to see. But when your love becomes routine and cools, your vision improves, and what would go unnoticed a few months earlier is now monumental and will affect the marriage for the rest of your lives.'"

"Did Granddad have any bad habits that annoyed you?"

"A few. And I had some that annoyed him. But we started out being open and honest with each other. If there was something that was a concern to the other, we discussed it, and if it was something we could change, we did. If not, we agreed to live with it. We felt that it was most important to get our differences out in the open before they became a problem. We started this long before we married. And if you had asked Bob about your suspicions, you would've had a better idea of the kind of person he is. Being able to communicate honestly and openly is the only way to establish a lasting relationship. And when you love someone as much as your grandfather and I did, the last thing you want is to offend or bring discomfort to the other."

"Sort of like Dad and me. There's no way I would've done something to cause him grief. I'm sure he felt the same. He respected me and always set a good example, and I was anxious to please. I agree that it's important to have someone you can express your opinion with, and they will be patient and listen. I feel very fortunate. First, I had Dad, and now I have you."

"As I see it," her grandmother began, "there's only one good thing about this ordeal with Bob—breaking up will be easier. Knowing he lied and cheated will upset you, but being angry will help you get over the hurt. Getting over the hurt is less difficult when you realize the guy is a jerk, and it sounds like he's one of the biggest."

"You're probably right. I think I'll go in my room and call Ruby. Maybe we can think of a way to get even."

"Don't concern yourself with getting even. You will find it to be a waste of time. Just forget him and go on with your life."

"I wish I could, but I can't, I have to get my revenge. Maybe I'll feel better when I make him regret he ever met me."

"Hi, Ruby."

"Hi, Angie. Did you find that I was telling the truth?"

"Yes. You knew I'd check, didn't you?"

"I thought you might. I know I would."

"I called his grandfather and found out that he isn't doing any remodeling."

"That bastard."

"I agree. Does Bob know that you know about me?"

"Not yet. I thought we could tell him together."

"That's a good idea. Does the ninth grader know about you and me?"

"No. But one of my girlfriends should have her name and phone number by tomorrow."

"Since I don't have a date with him tonight and I'm assuming you don't either, he must have a date with her."

"No doubt."

"He will more than likely, take her parking. Probably to the same place he told me was our special place."

"At the south end of Bradenton Beach, close to Longboat Pass?"

"Yes. Was that your special place?"

"That's what he told me."

"That bastard! What do you say we drive out and see if they're there?"

"What a super idea, Angie. I like the way you think. Where do you live? I'll come pick you up."

Since Ruby was a senior, Angie thought she would be intimidated. She wasn't. Ruby had a pretty face, a pleasant smile, and long brown hair—too long for her size; she was short and stocky. Her personality was her best feature, and it didn't take long before Angie thought of her as a friend, not her competition.

When they arrived at the beach, Ruby slowly drove toward the place they suspected he and his new girlfriend were parked: the same place both Angie and Ruby had lost their virginity.

Ruby was first to see his car. "There he is. The sorry bastard!"

"Yep. There the sorry bastard is. I like our new name we've given him."

"Me too."

Ruby pulled behind some trees and turned off the lights and then the engine. The silence was deafening. Angie sensed that Ruby was feeling the same anger and hurt as she. Neither said a word as they sat and looked at his car. It was parked in the same location that just the day before, Angie had thought of as Bob and her special spot. She couldn't help but think of how much she had loved him, how much she had enjoyed making love with him, and how much she was going to miss his affection. She thought of how it wasn't Bob she had loved—it was his lies. Also, because of his lies, she had willingly given up something very special.

Ruby started to open the door.

"Let's go confront them."

"Let's wait until we have a plan. I'd like to inform the other girl and give her the opportunity to join us when we confront him. Since he's not aware that we know about each other, let's do something he'll never forget but wish he could."

"What do you have in mind?"

"I don't know yet." She was silent for a moment. "You did say that tomorrow your friend will get this girl's name and phone number. Right?"

"Yes."

"I have an idea. I have a date with him tomorrow night. So you call this girl and tell her that you are Bob's friend and he had mentioned her to you. Tell her you and a few of his friends are putting on a surprise party for him at the beach, and you would like her to join in the surprise. That way, she won't tip him off. Then after you pick her up and are on your way to the beach, tell her what he's been up to."

By the time they arrived at Angie's house, the plan was finalized.

Being with Bob was extremely difficult, but Angie knew that for her scheme to have a chance of working, she had to act as if she enjoyed his company. She hoped for a hot night, and it was. On hot nights, he always left the engine running with the A/C on. Not only did they stay cool, the mosquitoes could not get to them.

She cringed each time he kissed her or tried to remove her clothes. While she stalled, she encouraged him to take off his clothes. Without being obvious, she constantly glanced out his rear window. Finally, she saw Ruby's headlights pull into the area where they were the night before. She removed the rest of her clothes.

He moved closer.

"I'm not feeling well," she said.

"Something must be wrong. You sure haven't been yourself tonight."

"I need a little fresh air. Let's go for a walk on the beach."

"Are you kidding? The mosquitoes will eat us alive."

"I have to get some fresh air or I'm going to be really sick."

"Okay. Let's get dressed."

"Oh no. Let's go out like this."

"Damn, Angie. You really want the mosquitoes to eat us."

"We won't be long. If you leave the engine running, the car will be nice and cool when we return. Come on, it'll be fun."

"Let's make it quick. You know how mosquito bites make me swell."

While walking on the beach, Angie covered her bare breasts with her arms and walked ahead of Bob; she wanted him to think she was looking at him when she looked back at the car. He was too busy flailing his arms at the mosquitoes to notice where she was looking.

Soon, the inside light of his car came on, then off. "I feel better now. Let's return to the car."

"Thank god. These mosquitoes are having their way with me."

He tried to open Angie's door for her, but it was locked. He accused her of locking her door, then went to the other side to open his. As soon as he walked away, she ran to meet Ruby. She heard him swearing at his locked door as she left.

Angie was relieved when she saw Ruby's lights come on and then pull up to her. Before she got in, Ruby got out and hollered, "Goodbye, sucker!"

Angie expressed her sentiments, "Goodbye, asshole!"

They high-fived before Ruby pulled away.

"Did you get everything?" Angie asked.

"Yes. Everything."

"Where are my clothes?" She hadn't noticed the girl in the back seat until her clothes were being handed to her. "Oh, hi. I'm Angie."

"Hi. I'm Gayle."

Ruby glanced at them. "I'm sorry. With all the excitement, I forgot to introduce you. Where does his grandfather live?"

"Straight ahead. I'll show you."

While Angie was putting on her clothes, she tried to make conversation with Gayle. But it was obvious that Gayle had been crying and was still too emotional to talk.

"I'm sorry you had to find out about him like this. I wish there had been more time to prepare you. I hope you're not upset with us."

"No. I'm not. I'm just hurt. Discovering that Bob is a lying jerk, and I loved him enough to give up my virginity, is difficult. And that's what I planned to do the next time we were together."

"We understand how you feel. The only difference is we didn't find out in time."

"That has to be bad. I want you both to know how much I appreciate you helping me not make a huge mistake. Thanks for caring enough to let me know."

"I'm glad you're looking at the situation like you are," Angie said. "I was afraid you'd be upset with us."

"No. I'm definitely not upset with you. I'd like to think I've made two new friends."

Angie and Ruby answered together, "You have."

While talking with Gayle, Angie couldn't help but notice her beautiful long blonde hair, her small attractive yet innocent face, and her petite body. It looked to Angie that she was no more than five feet tall and probably weighed less than a hundred pounds.

Angie continued to direct Ruby to Bob's grandfather's house, and by the time they arrived, she was dressed. Gayle stayed in the car; she didn't feel like getting out.

"Hi, Wayne."

"Hello, Angie."

"Wayne, this is Ruby."

"Nice meeting you, Ruby. What brings you girls to see me?"

Angie handed Bob's clothes to him. "We brought you Bob's clothes."

"Bob's clothes? What happened? Is he okay?"

"Except for many mosquito bites, he's fine. I feel certain he'll stop here to borrow some clothes before going home. So before you return these to him, wait and listen to his reason for not having them. He'll probably tell you he was robbed or something similar. But the truth is, when we discovered he was lying and seeing both of us at the same time, we had to get even. So I lured him out of his car while Ruby took his clothes and locked the doors. His wallet is in his pants, his underwear is there somewhere."

He smiled. "You mean he's naked?"

"Completely."

"Serves him right. And you're right. He won't tell me what really happened—this should be good. And I'm so sorry this happened to you girls."

"We are too," Angie said. "But I want you to know, I don't blame you. I feel certain you didn't know he was dating Ruby when you introduced us."

"I didn't, and I hope you believe me."

"I do. We better be going."

Before Ruby took Gayle home, Angie and Gayle exchanged phone numbers. Soon after Angie arrived home, Bob's grandfather called.

"Hi, Angie. You were right. He said he was robbed."

"Even though I thought he would, I can't believe he did."

"When he arrived, he was naked, had mosquito bites all over his body, and his ass was cut and bleeding from the little pieces of glass he sat on. The dumb ass didn't have enough sense to break the passenger window. He said he was driving through town when two men broke his window, stuck a gun in his face, got in his car, and told him to drive to the beach. Then they robbed him, made him take off his clothes, and stole them. He said he had no choice but to sit his naked ass in the glass on his seat. Then, because he didn't want his family and friends to see him naked, he drove straight here.

"I sympathetically and patiently waited until he finished telling me the interesting story he concocted. Then I got his clothes, handed them to him, and told him that you and Ruby were here earlier. He put his pants on and left without saying another word."

"I'm sorry, Wayne. It was wrong of me to get you involved."

"Don't be sorry. I'm glad you made me aware of what kind of boy he is. If I had known earlier, I would've been more cautious, and you wouldn't have had to go through what you did."

"I think we all learned a lot from this experience."

"I think you're right. I know I did. Good luck, Angie, and if I can ever help you with anything, let me know."

"Thanks. Take care."

Angie could hardly wait to call Ruby and let her know what Bob told his grandfather and what his grandfather told him. Then she called Gayle and told her. She decided to not mention any of what happened to her grandmother. If she said anything, her grandmother would figure out that she was sexually active, and she didn't want that.

It was late and she needed to get some sleep. After her shower, she went to bed but could not sleep. Her thoughts were about the evening and how she knew that Ruby, Gayle, Wayne, and even Bob were also lying awake. Then she thought of how embarrassed Bob must have been when his grandfather handed him his clothes. *I love it when a plan comes together.*

Later the next day, Gayle called.

"You'll never guess what happened."

"What?"

"Bob called. He said a window in his car was broken, and he couldn't go out with me tonight. I asked him how it broke. He said some men broke it and robbed him. He was surprised when I said, 'That's strange, it wasn't broken earlier last night.' He was silent for a moment, then said, 'How do you know? You weren't there.' I said, 'Oh, yes, I was. I was with Angie and Ruby.' And before I could say more, he hung up. Can you believe that idiot?"

"No, I can't. And now that I know him for what he is, I can't believe I fell for him."

Gayle paused before continuing, "I want to thank you again. I was about to make a mistake that can't be corrected. You opened my eyes, and from now on, I'll be a lot more cautious."

"I wish I had."

CHAPTER 6

Even though their ages and lifestyles were different, Angie, Ruby, and Gayle became close friends. Ruby got a job as hostess in a nice restaurant, Gayle babysat for a few of her parents' friends, and Angie began babysitting for a few more families.

Angie's babysitting jobs left her with little time for socializing but provided all the time she needed for homework; her grades reflected her dedication. Helping her grandmother with church activities also limited her free time. The advantage of staying busy was it helped take her mind off Bob and the humiliation she had suffered.

A few months after the fiasco with Bob, a new couple, Mr. and Mrs. White, joined the church Angie and her grandmother attended. They had a four-year-old daughter and were looking for a babysitter. Someone recommended Angie. Since most of the families she worked for needed her on weekends, and this family preferred weekdays, she agreed to babysit for them, but only on the nights and days her regular employers didn't need her.

The first night Angie arrived to babysit, she was surprised to see a young man in his late teens or early twenties there. Mrs. White said he was her husband's brother. He was attending college and living with them for a while. When he left the room, Angie approached the mother and quietly said, "I'm not comfortable with someone else here."

"Oh, don't worry. He'll be leaving soon after we leave."

Angie and Julie, the little girl, were sitting on the sofa reading a story when a door to an adjoining room opened and the young man joined them.

"Hi," he said. "We weren't properly introduced. My name is Burt."

She shook his hand without standing. "I'm Angie."

Burt went into the kitchen, opened a cabinet, and took out a bottle of vodka.

"How about I fix us a drink?"

"No thanks. I don't drink. And besides, I'm only sixteen."

"Ah, come on. Sixteen isn't too young. I started drinking when I was fourteen. We'll drink vodka. My brother has plenty. He'll never miss it, and no one will ever know. So how about having one?"

"No, thank you."

"One little drink won't hurt you. What do you say? Just one?"

"I'd rather not."

"I'll just mix you a weak one. Do you like orange juice?"

Angie realized she had to be stern. "I told you I don't want a drink, and I definitely don't want one while babysitting."

Without opening the bottle, Burt put it back in the cabinet, said goodbye, and left. After that first night when Angie came to babysit, Burt would leave soon after she arrived.

⁓

Angie had worked for the Whites several weeks when Mrs. White called and asked her to work on a night she was already scheduled to babysit.

"What am I going to do?" Mrs. White asked. "This is an important meeting my husband has to attend, and we were counting on you."

"I'm sorry, but I told you that I could only babysit for you on weekdays, and only if one of my regulars didn't need me. This is a weekend, and I'm already obligated. Sorry."

"Well, what am I supposed to do now!"

"I don't know." Then she thought of Gayle. "I have a friend that babysits. Maybe she won't be busy that night."

"Call her. And when you find out, call me back. I have to know one way or the other, and I have to know soon."

"The girl's name is Gayle, and if she's available, she'll call you. If not, I'll call you back."

"So I'll be hearing from one of you?"

"Right."

"Make it soon. Goodbye."

"Goodbye." *Wow! What a bitch. I've worked for her my last time. And I wish I hadn't told her about Gayle.*

〜

It was early when the people Angie was babysitting for returned home. On her way home, she stopped by the Whites to check on Gayle. As she started to ring the doorbell, she heard the door unlock, then watched as it slowly opened. It was Julie, the Whites' daughter.

"Hi, Julie. What are you doing up?"

"I couldn't sleep. I saw your lights when you pulled in the drive."

"Is Gayle sleeping?"

"I don't know."

"Well, where is she?"

"I don't know."

Thinking that her parents were home and one of them was taking Gayle home, she asked, "Are your parents home?"

"No."

She was beginning to worry.

"Is Burt home?"

"I think so."

The bottle of vodka and the open container of orange juice were the first things Angie saw. She ran toward Burt's bedroom door and, without knocking, flung it open. Burt was standing beside his bed; his pants were on, and he was in the process of pulling his T-shirt over his head. Gayle was lying on his bed, completely nude, and passed out. She wanted to scream at Burt but thought of Julie. Julie's mouth and eyes were wide open as she stared at Gayle.

"Come on, honey, let's go back to bed. Gayle is sick, but don't worry, I'll make her well."

Angie tucked Julie in. "I'm going to check on Gayle, but I'll be right back. Okay?"

"Okay."

Gayle was still nude and in the same position as when Angie first saw her. Burt had left. After covering Gayle and placing a wet washcloth on her head, Angie ran for the phone. She hoped to catch Ruby before she left work.

"Hi, Ruby."

"Angie. What's up?"

"We have a problem."

"What's our problem?"

"Gayle is sick and needs a ride home. Can you come get her?"

"Sure. I was just walking out the door when you called. Where are you?"

She gave Ruby the address. "There's more to the story than I can tell you now, so please hurry."

"I'll be right there."

Angie wet another washcloth with cold water and placed it around Gayle's throat, then rubbed her face with the one she placed on her head. When it felt warm, she wet it again and continued. She stopped when Gayle's eyelids began to twitch.

Gayle made a faint childlike moan, licked her lips, then slowly opened her eyes. "What happened? And where am I?"

"You're okay. Ruby's coming to take you home."

"Ruby is? Oh, yes. Now I remember. God, I feel sick."

"Do you feel like you're going to throw up?"

"Not yet. But it's developing." Her words were slurred, and Angie could barely make out what she was saying. "I'm so sorry, Angie. I really let you down, didn't I?"

"I don't know. Did you?"

"I guess I did. I have never had a drop of alcohol before tonight, and I had no idea that two drinks could make me feel this bad."

"You only had two?"

"Yes. Burt said he'd make them very weak."

"He lied. Did you have sex?"

"Are you kidding? Of course not!"

"Then why are you naked?"

"I'm naked?" She slowly, and with much effort, raised her head and lifted the sheet Angie had pulled over her. "Oh my god, Angie! What have I done?"

"Don't panic. You're still a virgin. When I came in, Burt was taking his clothes off, not putting them on."

With her eyes full of tears and her face full of sorrow, she raised her arms to Angie. They held each other tightly as Gayle shook and wept with uncontrollable emotion. She struggled with the words and finally managed to slur, "Oh, Angie. I feel so cheap. I'm so sorry."

"Don't worry about it. It's not your fault. Our main concern is getting you dressed and out of here before the Whites come home." Angie picked up Gayle's jeans that were on the floor and removed the sheet. "Let's just put your jeans and shirt on. We'll put your underwear in your purse." Angie pulled Gayle's jeans up both legs at the same time. "Lift up. Now let's see if you can sit up while I put your shirt on." She took Gayle's hands in hers and pulled her to a sitting position, then, with no help from Gayle and a lot of effort, began putting her shirt on. Angie compared it to dressing a helpless baby.

"Okay," Angie said. "Now let's go in the living room and wait for Ruby. She should be here any minute."

Angie was helping Gayle to a standing position when she heard a car pull into the driveway.

"There's Ruby. At least I hope it's Ruby. I better go check." She left Gayle in the bedroom while she went to the front door. "It's Ruby!"

"How sick is she?" Ruby asked.

"She's not sick. She's intoxicated."

"Intoxicated! Gayle?"

"Yes. I didn't want to tell you on the phone. I was afraid their daughter was listening."

"But…"

"We need to hurry and get her out of here before the parents get here. I'll tell you all about it later."

Ruby was shocked when she saw Gayle's condition. "Girl, girl, girl, you sure got yourself in a real mess."

"I know," Gayle slurred.

As they were helping Gayle to the car, Ruby asked, "Where am I taking her?"

"I don't know. I never thought of that. You can't take her home. We don't want her parents to see her in this condition."

"Yes. Take me home. My parents aren't there. They went camping."

"Good. Take her there, and I'll be over as soon as the Whites get home. I'll bring the rest of her clothes."

Angie rushed back in the house and quickly gathered up Gayle's shoes, socks, bra, panties, and purse, then took them out to her grandmother's car. At about the same time she had the kitchen cleaned and the vodka back in the cabinet, she heard a car pull in the driveway.

Wow! That was close.

"Where's Gayle?"

"On my way home, I stopped to see her. She wasn't feeling well, so I asked one of my friends to come get her and take her home."

"I hope it's nothing serious."

"She'll be fine." Mrs. White was buying her story. "She probably ate something that didn't agree with her."

Mrs. White handed Angie the money she had in her hand. "I'll give you the money. You and Gayle can divide it however you like."

⁓

The first thing Angie did when she arrived at Gayle's was call her grandmother.

"If it's okay with you, I'd like to spend the night with Gayle. She's not feeling well and her parents are out of town."

"That'll be fine. Just be home in time for church."

"I will. Thanks, Grandma. I'll see you in the morning."

Gayle was in bed with a wet washcloth on her head and Ruby was sitting beside her.

"How's she doing?" Angie asked.

"Not too good. She's thrown up twice and is on the verge of doing it again."

"I'll check their cabinets and see if they have any Alka-Seltzer. That'll help her. It always helped my mother." She located the Alka-Seltzer, plopped two in a small glass of water, and returned. "Let's sit her up so she can drink this."

Angie and Ruby sat with her on the edge of the bed, one on either side, and watched as she slowly sipped her medicine. When she finished, Angie took the glass and the three of them just sat without talking. They were hoping the medicine would work and waiting to see if it did.

After a few minutes, Gayle sat up straight and said, "I feel a little better." They smiled at each other and then had a group hug. Gayle lay back in bed. "I think I'm going to make it."

Angie returned the glass to the kitchen while Ruby wet the washcloth that was on Gayle's head with cold water, placed it back on her head, then wet another and placed it on her throat and chest.

Ruby and Angie were standing by her bed looking at her when Ruby asked, "What happened to her?"

"I'm not sure. She said she only had two drinks. They must've been extremely strong or Burt put something in them."

"Who's Burt?"

"He's the jerk who lives there, the husband's brother. I know he talked her into having a drink because the first night I babysat for them, he tried to get me to have one. He got mad when I refused."

"What an idiot! Was he there when you arrived?"

"Yes. He was standing beside his bed, taking his clothes off. Gayle was lying on the bed, passed out and naked."

"Oh my god!" Ruby said. "Are you sure he was taking his clothes off?"

"Yes. His T-shirt was over his head and he was pulling it off."

"Thank you, Jesus!" Ruby looked at Gayle. "You're a lucky girl."

Tears were running down each side of Gayle's face, and her chin began to tremble. Without opening her eyes, she nodded and whispered, "I know."

Angie lay beside her, Gayle moved to the middle, and Ruby lay on the other side. Still in their clothes and each with an arm over Gayle, they cuddled up and fell asleep.

The sun was high and they were still lying in almost the same position. Angie propped her head up on her hand and removed the washcloth from Gayle's head and the one from her neck. Gayle opened her eyes and smiled.

Angie returned her smile. "Good morning. How do you feel?"

"Weak and shaky, but much better."

Ruby was waking.

"Good morning," Angie and Gayle said.

"Good morning." She blinked her eyes a few times, then looked at Gayle. "How do you feel?"

"Much better."

"Good."

"Well, guys," Angie said as she stretched, "I hate to be a party pooper, but I have to get my grandmother's car back to her so she can go to church."

Ruby looked at her watch. "I better call my parents and let them know I'll be here a few more hours. I'll use the phone in the kitchen."

Angie helped Gayle to a sitting position, then placed the pillows behind her. Gayle pulled her long blonde hair over her shoulder and lay back against the pillows. Angie sat beside her and watched as she adjusted the pillows to a more comfortable position. With her eyes closed, Gayle slowly allowed her head to relax; it was as if opening her eyes or moving her head too quickly would be painful.

Angie admired Gayle's petite features and wondered how a man as large as Burt could think of taking advantage of such a small innocent-looking girl. Several weeks before, Gayle had told Angie her weight; it was only eighty-five pounds.

Gayle's eyes were still closed when a small smile began to form; she opened them and saw that Angie was smiling with her.

"Well, Angie, you guys have literally saved my ass again."

They laughed, then hugged. "You are making it difficult for Ruby and me to preserve your virginity."

"That was close. Thanks for stopping to check on me. And I really appreciate all you've done."

"I'm glad I stopped. I'd hate to think of what could've happened if I hadn't got there when I did."

"Me too."

"I have to run. Try to eat something. You need to get your strength back. I'll come back and check on you when my grandmother returns from church." Angie waved to Ruby as she started to leave; she was still on the phone. "I'll be back as soon as I can."

"I'll be here."

"How's Gayle?" Angie's grandmother asked.

"She's doing much better. I'll check on her again when you come home from church if I can borrow your car?"

"Sure. What do you think made her sick?"

Angie had never lied to her grandmother, and she was not going to start. She had to word her answer without lying but not telling the whole truth. "Probably something she ate or drank."

"It could be a virus."

"Maybe."

"I'll see you after church."

Angie normally attended church with her grandmother, but on those days she chose to not go, her grandmother never insisted or made her feel guilty. Angie didn't agree with the teachings of her grandmother's church and definitely didn't care for the snobbish, inconsiderate members. Even though her feelings were obvious, they were never discussed.

After a light breakfast of toast and milk, Angie took a shower. While getting dressed, the phone rang.

"Angie?"

"Yes."

"Let me speak to your grandmother!"

"She's not here. She's at church. Who is this?"

"This is Beverly White. I can't believe you recommended Gayle to babysit my daughter. You lied to me last night. You said she was sick, when in reality, she was drunk. Julie said she saw Gayle on Burt's bed. And she was naked! I asked Burt what happened. He said she was fine when he left, but when he returned, she was on his bed, passed out, and naked. He was trying to wake her when you came in. He said he left soon after so you and Gayle could have some privacy. Why am I telling you this? You know what happened!"

"That's not—"

"I don't want to hear anything you have to say. I'll call back later and let your grandmother know what Gayle did and how you lied and covered for her."

"I'd like to explain—"

Click.

Angie's hand was shaking so much she could hardly dial Gayle's number. Ruby answered.

"We have a big problem."

"Bigger than last night?"

"Much bigger. That bitch, Beverly White, called and is accusing Gayle of being responsible for what happened last night."

"You have to be kidding!"

"I wish I were. She hung up on me without letting me explain. I have to get over there and make her listen before she tells my grandmother."

"I'll be right there."

Angie wasn't sure she would be back before her grandmother returned, so she wrote a note letting her know she was with Ruby. It took only a few minutes for Ruby to arrive, but it seemed to Angie as if it were an hour. The thought of confronting Beverly White had her so nervous she felt sick. Her legs were weak and trembling as she walked to Ruby's car. While fastening her seat belt, she said, "This should be fun."

"How did she find out?"

"Julie, her daughter, told her that she saw Gayle on Burt's bed and her clothes were off."

"Did she?"

"Yes."

"Bummer."

"How's Gayle?"

"She was doing pretty good until she heard me talking to you. She wanted to come with us, but I told her it would only upset her, and she didn't need that. She really feels bad about what she did and getting us involved."

"I know."

Ruby parked in the driveway. Angie looked for Burt's car, but it wasn't there. With their eyes fixed on the house, Angie asked, "Do you want to come with me?"

"There's nothing I'd rather do." They smiled as they opened their doors.

Angie could feel her finger trembling as she pushed the button for the doorbell. Beverly opened the door.

"What do you want?"

"I would like to talk with you and explain what happened."

"I don't want to listen to any more of your lies. And you and Gayle are going to be in a lot of trouble when I tell your grandmother and her parents."

Ruby had less control of her temper than Angie and was about to lose it. "Are you afraid to talk with her?"

"Who are you?"

"I'm her attorney."

"You have a smart mouth."

"And you are an arrogant bitch!"

Mr. White came from behind Beverly. "You can't talk to my wife like that!"

Beverly gave him a stern look. "Shut up, Harold, I'll handle this."

Ruby looked at Angie and, loud enough for Harold to hear, said, "Not only is she arrogant, she wears the pants."

Beverly looked at Angie and began closing the door. "Your smart-mouth friend has insulted me all she's going to! Now get off my property!"

Before Beverly could get the door completely closed, Angie shouted, "You'll talk to me or I'm going to the sheriff!"

The door swung open and Beverly's face was red with rage. "What do you mean, *you'll* go to the sheriff?"

"Just what I said! Now, let us in!"

Beverly backed away from the door enough for them to pass. "I want to hear this."

Ruby glared at Beverly as she passed. "I don't think you do."

Angie was so nervous she could hardly talk, but she knew she had to say what she came to say. "It was wrong of Gayle to drink while babysitting, but—"

Beverly butted in, "There's no but to it. And if you came here to apologize for Gayle and are thinking I'll forgive and forget, you're badly mistaken. I haven't heard you tell me you're sorry for lying, and even if you do, I'm still going to tell your grandmother."

"I'm not going to apologize, and neither is Gayle."

"Then we have nothing else to talk about. Now get out of my house!"

"I'm not leaving until I've said what I came to say."

Beverly moved toward Angie. "Oh yes, you are!"

Ruby got between them. "Why don't you just shut up and listen! I'm beginning to think you're afraid you're going to hear something you don't want to hear. Tell her, Angie."

"Burt is just as much to blame as Gayle. In fact, he's more to blame."

Beverly started toward them again. "Now you're bringing Burt into this. I've heard enough of your lying. Get out!"

Her husband stepped between them. "I want to hear what Angie has to say."

"Stay out of this, Harold!"

"No. I'm not. Now let Angie talk."

"The first night I babysat for you, Burt tried to get me to have a drink with him. When I refused, he became more persistent. He offered to make it very weak and with vodka. He said, that way, no one would know. I told him I was sixteen. He said he was fourteen when he started drinking. Finally, when he was convinced I wasn't going to have a drink, he got mad, put the bottle of vodka back in the cabinet, and left. I guess Gayle couldn't convince him and believed what he said about making them weak."

"That's a lie. Why was she in his bed with her clothes off?"

"He put her there, and he took off her clothes."

"That's the biggest lie yet. He wouldn't do that."

Angie looked down the hall and saw Julie standing around the corner.

"Harold?" she asked.

"Yes."

"Can I ask Julie a question?"

"Sure." He looked down the hall where Angie was looking. "Julie, honey, come here, please. Angie wants to ask you a question."

Angie knelt down beside her.

"Hi, Julie."

"Hi, Angie."

"You're a smart little girl, and your memory is much better than mine. Did you see Burt pour Gayle some orange juice?"

"Yes."

"What did he do after he gave Gayle the orange juice?"

"He told me it was my bedtime. So I went to bed."

"Do you remember what Burt was doing when you and I went into his room last night?"

"Yes."

"What was he doing?"

"He was taking his shirt off."

"Are you sure he was taking it off, not putting in on?"

"He was pulling it off over his head. I remember."

Ruby didn't take her eyes off Beverly while Angie talked with Julie. She watched as Beverly's eyes turned red and filled with tears and how her hands trembled as she put them over her open mouth. Ruby continued to evaluate Beverly's actions as Angie thanked Julie and complimented her for being so smart. It was obvious that Beverly was hearing something she really didn't want to hear and was about to burst with emotion. Ruby was suspicious.

Beverly turned her back to everyone, walked to the sofa and sat down, put her face in her hands, and wept uncontrollably.

"Why! Why! Why! How could he do this to me?"

Ruby lost what little control she had. "I knew it!"

Harold turned and looked at his wife. "To you!"

"I mean, us."

"I think you're too emotional to mean us. I think you meant you. I've suspected for some time that you and Burt were up to something, now I'm certain."

Angie took Julie by the hand. "Let's go to your room and play with your toys."

Angie closed Julie's door, then began talking loudly about her toys.

Ruby joined them. "I think we should be going."

"I know we should, but I hate to leave Julie."

Julie's eyes expressed her sadness as she looked at Angie.

"I'll be okay. I'm used to their fighting. I'll just stay in my room like I always do."

Angie and Ruby looked at each other; their eyes were red and filled with tears.

Ruby bent down and hugged Julie. "You're a brave girl. I'm glad I met you."

"It was nice meeting you, Ruby."

Angie kissed her on the cheek. "Goodbye, Julie."

"Goodbye, Angie."

As they walked past Harold and Beverly, Ruby said to Angie, "Our work here is done."

"Yes, it is."

It was a quiet ride to Gayle's. The memory of Julie prevented them from rejoicing.

CHAPTER 7

That summer, Angie turned seventeen and Ruby graduated. Since Ruby wasn't attending school and was eighteen, she became a full-time waitress instead of a part-time hostess. When Ruby knew she was going to become a waitress, she recommended Angie for her replacement. The restaurant was large, and Angie joined several other high school students who worked there. Everything came together perfectly: Ruby made a lot more money, Gayle took over Angie's babysitting commitments, and Angie loved her new job.

When Angie informed the families she worked for that she would no longer be babysitting, one family asked if she would like to buy their '66 Mustang convertible. They no longer needed three cars, and knowing that Angie had expressed more than a casual interest in it, they wanted her to have first refusal.

Angie was thrilled that the owners had thought of her first, and $1,400 was an exceptionally good buy, especially in its condition. The top had recently been replaced, and there wasn't a blemish in the highly waxed and polished bright-red finish. The husband told her he bought it from his father, and his father bought it new; it was obvious that both had given it a lot of TLC.

After mentioning how much she appreciated them thinking of her, she told them that she would love to own it. All she had to do was come up with the money. She only had $400 saved.

I'll have to get a loan.

The thought of owning her own car had her so excited she could hardly drive her grandmother's car home; she thought how it might be the last time she had to use it. Even though her grandmother had never refused her when she asked to borrow her car, she realized how much of an inconvenience it had been. *Owning my own car will not only benefit me but Grandma too.* She was anxious to get home with the news.

Her grandmother seemed pleased when she told her about the car, but Angie was shocked when she heard her say, "It sounds like a good car and a great deal, but I won't go on a note for you."

"Really? But why?"

"I have a better idea. Almost every month, I've saved $50 of your Social Security check. I've been looking forward to the day you need something special, and it looks to me like that day has come. You have $2,500. Now, let's go see your new car."

Tears were in Angie's eyes as she hugged and thanked her grandmother.

By the time Angie and her grandmother took the car for a drive and checked it out, it was too late that night to close the deal, so Angie told the owners to expect her early the next morning.

After buying the Mustang, tag, insurance, and paying the sales tax, Angie had $800 left of the $2,500 her grandmother had given her. She added it to the $400 she had in savings.

The first thing Angie did, after taking care of all that was required with purchasing a car, was to let the top down and take her grandmother for a ride. They stopped at the mall, did a little shopping, had lunch, then back to just riding around, their hair blowing in the wind. Angie was thrilled with her car. She loved driving it and it showed; she could hardly keep from smiling. She was just as delighted that her grandmother was enjoying her car and the day as much as she. They drove, laughed, and joked until it was time for Angie to get ready for work. Spending the day with her grandmother while driving around in her sporty car was a memory that would never be forgotten.

Angie

Most days that summer, Ruby, Gayle, and Angie spent their mornings on the beach. On the days it was too hot for the beach and before it was time for Ruby and Angie to start work, they went shopping or just drove around.

They stayed close until summer was almost over. That's when Ruby found, as she described him, "the perfect man." He worked at the same restaurant as Ruby and Angie. His hours and Ruby's were the same, and they were together every available minute. The only time Angie and Ruby saw each other or spent time together was at work, and when Angie returned to school, they spent even less time together. Angie and Gayle stayed close, and even though they missed being with Ruby, they were pleased that she found someone she cared for and someone who truly cared for her.

It was obvious to everyone, especially the manager, that Angie loved her job. There had been several times when the manager had complimented her and expressed his appreciation for the caring, enthusiastic effort she made to please the customers; he had proudly watched as they were greeted by her large beautiful smile, how she rarely forgot a returning customer, and how legitimately pleased she was to see them.

He was also impressed with the way she greeted the children. She always knelt down to their level and complimented them on something: it could be their hair, eyes, teeth, smile, clothing, or even their shoes, but always something. She would ask their names and tell them hers, then stand and walk with the children, not the parents, while directing them to their table. She never walked ahead; she walked with and asked questions and talked with them as she did. After a few return visits, the children, and most of the adults, called her by name. Most of the time, she remembered theirs.

Several of the other young girls who worked as hostesses tried to imitate Angie, but it was obvious to the customers that they were faking, and their actions came across as phony. Angie's charm and personality were difficult to imitate. She was a natural.

Angie looked older than she was, so no one close to her age asked her for a date. She was asked out many times, but always by men in their twenties or thirties, and occasionally by someone who had been in a few days earlier with their wife. She found it difficult to control her composure when a married man asked her out.

She envied the pleasure and happiness that Ruby and her boyfriend enjoyed. It caused her to miss not having someone special in her life—someone to love and be loved by and someone to make love with. Often, she would lay awake yearning to be satisfied, but she was aware of her priorities and wasn't going to give in to her desires, which could possibly affect her chances for a scholarship. For now, just keeping up with all she had to do was occupying all her time. She had convinced herself that this was the way her life would be until she graduated.

Even if I find Mr. Right, I won't have time to go out.

The only other activity she was involved with was church, and only because of the love and respect she had for her grandmother. Even on the Sundays she worked, which was every fourth Sunday, she attended church that morning before going to work. Angie worked most days from 4:00 p.m. until 9:00 p.m. and every Saturday from 11:00 a.m. until 9:00 p.m. That left little time to spend with her grandmother, but the time they shared was valued. It seemed that during the week and after church, her grandmother was always helping someone in need.

On the Sundays Angie didn't have to work, she helped her grandmother care for her sick or disabled friends. After delivering the food they had prepared, they looked around to see what else they could help with. If their house needed cleaning, they cleaned it; if their clothes or dishes needed washing, they washed them. They would even change and wash the bed linens if they needed changing and do whatever else they saw that needed doing. Angie admired her grandmother for being the caring person she was and enjoyed helping her.

One Sunday, Angie and her grandmother noticed that Wayne wasn't at church. They heard someone say he was getting over a hernia operation. They were concerned and wondered if there was anything they could do for him. Angie's grandmother didn't want to call—she said it might give him the wrong impression—so she asked Angie.

"Hi, Wayne. This is Angie."

"Angie. It's so good to hear your voice. How are you and Maxine doing?"

That was the first time she had heard him call her grandmother by name.

"From what we hear, we're doing much better than you. How are you feeling?"

"I guess you heard I had a hernia operation?"

"Yes, we did."

"The operation was no problem. It's the staph infection I contracted while in the hospital that's about to drive me crazy."

"That's too bad. Is your family or someone helping you?"

"No. I haven't seen anyone and don't expect to."

Angie's grandmother was getting the drift of the conversation. "Ask if he would like some homemade vegetable soup."

"Grandma wants me to ask if you'd like some homemade vegetable soup?"

"I'd love some. But I can't let you see my house in the condition it's in. I haven't felt like cleaning. Were you planning to bring it today?"

"Yes. As soon as she makes it."

"Will you mind if I meet you at the door? I'd rather you not see how I've neglected my housework."

"I understand. We'll call before we leave and you can meet us at the door."

"Thanks, Angie."

They called, but Angie knew her grandmother wasn't going to let Wayne get away with not letting them in.

Wayne was dressed in his housecoat and slippers. "Hi, ladies."

"Hello, Wayne," they answered. "How are you feeling?"

"A little better. Your call perked me up. Here, let me take that."

"Oh no," Maxine said as she eased past him. "You don't need to be carrying this heavy pot of hot soup. I'll take it in and put it on the stove."

"Please don't look at my house. I'm really ashamed of the way it looks."

"We won't." She placed the pot of soup on the stove and turned the burner on warm. Angie followed her in with the rolls and some other food they brought. "How about Angie and I heat the rolls and have a bowl of soup with you?"

"I'd like that. But I'm not sure I have enough clean bowls."

"You find a comfortable chair and relax. Angie and I will take care of everything."

Angie helped him to his lounge chair, lifted the footrest, put a pillow under his head, then asked if there was anything she could get him. He said he was fine, but by the yearning look in his eyes, she knew he wanted something. "Can I mix you a drink?"

"Oh, god, Angie, would you?"

"Sure. What can I get you?"

"Wild Turkey on the rocks."

Angie was pleased when her grandmother smiled as she prepared Wayne's drink. It was as if she had accepted his drinking, at least for the day.

Wayne was licking his lips as Angie walked toward him. He reached for the drink with both hands, and while still holding it with both hands, he took a long, pleasurable sip. "Thank you, Angie. You're an angel."

Angie's grandmother hand-washed enough bowls and spoons for their soup while Angie loaded the dishwasher with the dishes piled in the sink. When they finished, they joined Wayne. They had agreed to add the soup bowls and turn on the dishwasher before they left.

When Angie and her grandmother had the kitchen squared away, they joined Wayne in the living room. Before Angie sat, she noticed there was nothing but ice in Wayne's glass. As she reached for his glass, he looked up and smiled, then handed her his empty glass. He thanked her when she returned with a fresh drink.

Angie was afraid Wayne would mention her episode with Bob, but he didn't. She figured he knew she had not told her grandmother.

It surprised Angie to see how tolerant her grandmother was with Wayne's drinking and how she was almost flirting with him during their conversations. To give her grandmother and Wayne some time alone, Angie put the rolls in the oven and set the table.

After dinner, Wayne went back to his lounge chair, Angie added the bowls to the dishwasher, and while she cleaned the kitchen, her grandmother joined Wayne. He lifted his hand from his chair, encouraging her to come to him. She moved closer, held his hand in both of hers, and asked, "How are you feeling?"

"As good as new. Thanks to you and Angie. Your soup was delicious."

"Thanks."

"You are a good cook." With his eyes fixed on hers, he said, "I would like to be your friend, Maxine. Not because you're a good cook, but because you're a wonderful person."

"You do?"

"Yes. A close friend."

"We'll see. For now, let's just concentrate on getting you well." She was getting embarrassed and anxious to change the subject. "I put the rest of the soup in the refrigerator, so when you're ready for some more, you can dip it into a bowl and warm it in the microwave. I'll call and check on you occasionally."

"You and Angie have changed what started out as a depressing day into a wonderful day, one I'll always remember. I appreciate what you've done more than I can express. Thank you."

⌒◌

True to her word, Angie's grandmother called Wayne almost every day. And when he was well enough, he asked her out to dinner. They chose the restaurant where Angie worked, and from time to time, she joined them at their table. As she listened to their conversation, it was obvious that Wayne and her grandmother had nothing in common and he was bored. A man as worldly as Wayne required more topics to discuss than religion and sick friends. Even though that night was the last time he asked her out, they kept in touch and remained close friends.

CHAPTER 8

On a Sunday Angie didn't have to work and two weeks before Christmas, Angie and her grandmother were putting up and decorating their Christmas tree. They were also planning Christmas dinner.

"Will you be asking Wayne to join us?" Angie asked.

"Yes. I think we should. Don't you?"

"Yes, I do."

Angie continued to fuss with the tree; her grandmother was sitting in her favorite chair, admiring their work.

"He seemed to enjoy last Christmas with us," her grandmother said. "I know I enjoyed having him. You know? Wayne is an awfully nice man. I just wis'…he…wou'…n't…driiink…so…musss."

Thinking that her grandmother was saying something humorous, Angie laughed, then turned to comment. Her grandmother's head had fallen forward; her chin was resting on her chest.

"Grandma! What's wrong?" Shock, fear, and grief rushed through her as she lifted her grandmother's head and saw her distorted face.

"Grandma! Grandma! What's happening?" She hugged her, then ran for the phone, called 911, then hurried back. When Angie saw the fear in her grandmother's pleading eyes, she lost control of her emotions and began crying loudly. She held her and cried until the ambulance arrived. She didn't know what else to do.

"It looks like she's having a stroke," the paramedic said. "We have to hurry."

When Angie saw there was not enough room in the ambulance for her, she ran to her car.

"I'll follow you in my car."

The nurse stopped Angie at the door. "You'll have to wait in the lobby. I'll keep you informed of her condition. In the meantime, you need to fill out some papers with the lady at the desk."

While Angie filled out the forms, it dawned on her that she didn't know who to notify. The only living relative her grandmother had mentioned was a sister who lived somewhere in Texas. *Grandma will want her minister to know, but who else? She really doesn't have any close friends. Let's see. First thing in the morning, I'll call where she works, after that, the minister, and later, I'll call my boss.*

She stood when she saw the nurse walking toward her.

"Your grandmother is in the Intensive Care Unit. I wish I could let you see her, but I can't, not for a while. Are you the only one caring for her?"

"Yes."

"Then since you can't see her tonight and it's two o'clock, I suggest you go home and get some sleep. You'll need the rest. Her doctor will want to talk with you in the morning, so try to return around eight."

"I'll be here."

Her tears made the streetlights and the headlights from the few oncoming cars appear to be large, out of focus, glittering balls. She blinked often, with little results. The red fuzzy glow of the traffic light seemed to fill her car as she waited and wondered why it took so long to change, especially when there were no cars in any direction. As she sat with both hands on top of the steering wheel, looking at the blurred light, and feeling the tears streaming down her cheeks, she began to feel guilty and wished she had not left her grandmother. Her throat and chest ached with grief and she shook with emotion. She dropped her forehead onto the back of her hands and wept. *What if she gets worse and I'm not there? I'd never forgive myself.*

She glanced up at the light; it was green, but she didn't move. With her head back on her hands, she continued to cry. *I better go back. But what can I do? The nurse is right. I should get some sleep. I need to be alert when I talk with the doctor.* The light had changed to red. She dried her eyes and cheeks with her hands, which didn't help, then waited for the light to change again.

"Your grandmother had a stroke," the doctor said. "I won't know the extent of her disability until I review the results of the test and observe her for a few days. I do know it's her right side that's affected. To what degree I don't know, we'll just have to wait and see. I understand that you're the one, and possibly the only one, caring for her."

"Yes, that's true."

"How old are you, Angie?"

"I'm seventeen."

"Are you still in school?"

"Yes. A senior."

"Going to school and taking care of your grandmother is going to be quite difficult. I suggest you get a family member or someone to help you."

"The only relative she has, besides me, is a sister in Texas, but I'm sure that some of the members of her church will help."

"That's good because I feel you're going to need help, maybe even professional help. But I'm getting ahead of myself. Let's wait and see how she progresses. She may not be impaired as much as I suspect. Angie, I'm not trying to alarm you, but you need to prepare yourself for the worst."

"I will, and thanks for being concerned. Can I see her?"

"Yes, but only for a few minutes. She's still in the Intensive Care Unit. She's sleeping, which is what she needs, so please try to not wake her."

A voice from behind them said, "I'll go with you."

They turned around—it was the minister from the church that she and her grandmother attended. Angie introduced him to the doctor, then the doctor escorted them into the ICU. As they stood beside her bed, the minister said, "Let us pray."

His voice grew louder: Angie opened her eyes just in time to see the doctor grasp the minister by the arm, then pull him toward the door. She followed them out.

When they were in the hall, the doctor turned to him and, in a demanding voice, said, "I really think a quiet prayer will do as much good as a loud one. She needs her sleep, and you need to learn how to pray a little quieter."

The minister gave the doctor a look of disbelief, a look that questioned the doctor's authority to discipline a man representing the Lord. He stopped making eye contact and lowered his head when he noticed the doctor wasn't impressed.

The doctor turned to Angie, smiled, and said, "I'll see you later today."

Without even glancing at the minister, he hastily walked away.

Angie saw the minister shake his head as his eyes followed the doctor. Instead of comforting her and without saying another word, he left her standing just outside the door leading to her critically ill grandmother. She had always disliked her grandmother's church and its followers, and now she cared even less for the minister.

Once Angie realized there was nothing she could do to help her grandmother by staying at the hospital, she returned home. She called her school and informed them of her situation. Fortunately, there was only a week left before the two-week Christmas vacation started. The manager at the restaurant where she worked told her to take all the time she needed and keep him informed of her grandmother's condition. Earlier, before leaving for the hospital, she had called her grandmother's employer.

After making the beds, cleaning the house, and eating a sandwich, Angie returned to the hospital. The nurse told her that her grandmother's condition had not changed and the doctor would be in later to talk with her. She took a seat in the waiting room. It seemed like several hours, but it was only a few before the doctor arrived.

"Hi, Angie. I'm pleased to say that your grandmother's condition is not as acute as I originally thought, but it's still serious. She has lost about 50 percent use of her right arm and leg, and as you've seen, her face and mouth are disfigured. I suspect you won't be able to understand what she's saying, but fortunately, she's left-handed and should be able to communicate by writing. She won't be able to walk without the use of a walker, at least for a while. She may always have to use a walker. Let's see. Today is Monday, so we'll probably start rehabilitation treatments on Wednesday or Thursday. The therapists will teach her how to use a walker and a lot more."

"Can I see her?"

"Yes, but only for a short while. I want to keep her in the ICU one more night, and if she continues to improve, she'll be moved in the morning into a semiprivate room. This time of year, the hospital has only a few patients, so she'll have a room to herself. Since she'll be alone, you can visit with her as often as you like and stay as long as you like."

"Thanks."

Angie was careful to approach her grandmother on the left side. They made eye contact, her grandmother lifted her hand, and Angie rushed to caress it. She felt her grandmother squeeze her hands as she held her hand with both hers. Neither said a word as they watched the tears building in the other's eyes. Angie was trying with all her strength to control her emotions. She didn't want her grandmother to see her cry, but her chin began to quiver when she saw the tears flowing down both sides of her grandmother's distorted face. She felt her own tears falling on her hands. She had to regain her composure.

It was difficult, and the words were forced. "The doctor tells me that you'll be getting your own room in the morning. They won't let me visit with you much in here, but when they move you, I'll be able to spend as much time with you as I want." She felt her grandmother give her hand a little squeeze. "The nurse wants me to leave now, but I'll be here early in the morning."

Angie waved from the doorway, then rushed to the nearest restroom. She was sobbing even before she entered. While holding her face in a wet paper towel, she continued to cry. After several minutes, she removed the towel, wet it again, and placed it back on her face. As she concentrated on the cool towel against her face, her crying began to subside. It was several more minutes before she dried her face, fixed her makeup, and left.

🙦

The phone was ringing as Angie was unlocking the door. It was Ruby.

"The manager just told me that your grandmother had a stroke."

"Yes, she did."

"Will she be okay?"

"I'm not sure. Her doctor said he'd know more in a few days."

"Oh, Angie. I'm so sorry. Is there anything I can help you with?"

"I can't think of anything."

"I'll be checking on you, but in the meantime, promise me you'll let me know if there's anything I can do."

"I will."

"No, you won't. Now promise me."

"I promise."

"I have to get back to work. I'll call you tomorrow."

🙦

Angie was sitting in a chair beside her grandmother's bed. She had gotten there early and was waiting for her when she arrived from the ICU. Her grandmother had tried to talk several times, but her words were garbled, so Angie did all the talking. As she rambled, she noticed that her grandmother was trying to say something. She stopped talking and listened intensely but couldn't understand her words. After a few minutes of trying, her grandmother raised her left hand and, with her fingers, made a motion as if she was writing.

"Oh, you want to write something."

Her grandmother nodded.

Angie went to the nurses' station and returned with a clipboard and pen. She handed the pen to her grandmother and held the clipboard so she could write, then watched as she wrote.

Good morning.

"Good morning."

What day is it?

"Tuesday."

Are you okay?

"I'm fine. But I'm not the one we need to be concerned with. You're the one that's had a temporary setback. And we need to concentrate on getting you well and back home. We have a Christmas to prepare for."

I don't think it's temporary.

"We'll see."

Later in the afternoon, three nice flower arrangements were delivered. Angie read the cards: "This one is from where you work, this one is from my work, and this one is from your church. Your minister was here when you were in the ICU. He said a prayer for you."

She picked up the pen, and Angie held the clipboard.

How did he know?

"I called him."

Thank you.

"Hi, ladies."

Angie turned to see that the doctor had entered the room.

"Good afternoon."

"I have good news." He didn't wait for a response. "We are going to start therapy tomorrow morning."

"Great! Do you think she'll be able to go home before Christmas?"

"Let's see how her therapy goes. I'll know more in a couple days."

The doctor asked Angie's grandmother some yes and no questions; she answered by nodding or shaking her head. When the doctor finished and had left, she held up her hand and made the writing sign with her fingers. Angie took the clipboard to her.

I'll be in therapy tomorrow. You go to school.

"Are you sure?"

She nodded.

"Okay. But I'll be here as soon as school lets out."

OK.

For the remainder of the week, Angie went to school, then returned and stayed with her grandmother until visiting hours were over.

That Saturday, before Angie woke, Ruby and Gayle were at her house. They came to help decorate the Christmas tree that she and her grandmother were working on when her grandmother had the stroke. When they finished the tree, they decorated the house, then went with Angie to visit her grandmother. They had other obligations and couldn't stay long, but their stay was long enough to realize that Angie and her grandmother had a rough road ahead.

Early the next morning, Angie woke to the sound of someone knocking on her door. It was Ruby and Gayle. They took her to Ruby's favorite restaurant for breakfast; Angie took her car so she could go straight from the restaurant to the hospital. Ruby and Gayle accompanied her to the hospital but did not stay long; Ruby had to work that afternoon and Gayle had to babysit.

The room fell silent; Angie could tell that her grandmother had enjoyed Ruby and Gayle's company, and now, just like her, she missed the sound of their voices and their laughter.

Angie was surprised that when the day was over, only two members of their church came to visit. *I hope no one else comes to visit. Maybe then Grandma will realize just how inconsiderate the whole congregation is and find another church to attend.*

It was Monday, Christmas vacation had started, and there was no school for the next two weeks. Angie arrived at the hospital early; she didn't want to miss seeing the doctor.

The doctor smiled as Angie entered her grandmother's room. "Hi, Angie. I was just telling your grandmother that if she continues to improve, she can go home Thursday morning."

Angie had moved to her grandmother's side and was holding her hand. "It looks like we'll be cooking that turkey for Christmas dinner after all." Angie felt her hand being squeezed, and her throat began to tighten when her grandmother's eyes expressed her joy and her lips formed a little half smile. She quickly turned back to the doctor. "Thank you."

"Someone from therapy will be talking with you. They'll teach you how to care for your grandmother. They'll also arrange a time that's convenient for you to have whatever rails and other devices you'll need installed in your home." He was standing on the opposite side of the bed from Angie and looking at her grandmother. "Now, I'm going to explain to you what damage the stroke has caused and what to expect. As you know, you've lost about 50 percent use of your right arm and leg. I doubt they'll ever return to the way they were, but with the proper exercise and therapy, they will improve. Your face will be difficult for therapy to improve, but I do know that therapy will help your speech. So it's most important that you work with your therapist and keep your appointments."

"We will. Won't we, Grandma?"

She nodded.

He turned to Angie. "Since you're going to be the only one caring for her, I want to be sure you understand what your responsibilities will be. Until she's more familiar with her walker, you'll have to help her get around. You may have to help her in and out of the bathroom for a while, but she'll be able to take care of herself when using the toilet. Do you have a bathtub or a shower?"

"Both. Actually, they're together."

"The man that installs the rails will also provide a stool for her to sit on while taking a shower. Even with the rails, she'll need help getting in and out of the tub and probably some help bathing. Are you going to be comfortable with that?"

"Yes. No problem. Right, Grandma?"

She nodded.

"It's most important that someone be with her until she can maneuver her walker."

"I understand, and I'll be with her."

"You will let Angie know if you need something that's difficult to get or difficult to do, right?"

She nodded.

"Good luck. And if you have any questions, give me a call."

CHAPTER 9

By Thursday, the hand rails at the entrance of the house, around the toilet, and on the wall of the shower and bathtub had been installed. A stool was in the tub and a handheld shower was also installed. It was mid-afternoon and Angie had just gotten her grandmother home and in bed when the phone rang. It was Gayle.

"Ruby and I have a good idea, at least we think it's a good idea. How about if we come over early Christmas morning, help you prepare dinner, and spend the day with you and your grandmother?"

"That's a wonderful idea!"

"Good. We'll be there tomorrow morning before Ruby goes to work. We'll make a list of the things we need, then return Saturday morning and start cooking."

"I wasn't looking forward to Christmas day, but thanks to you and Ruby, I am now."

"We're pretty excited too. We don't know as much about cooking as you, so we're counting on you and Grandma to teach us."

Angie smiled. That was the first time she heard Gayle refer to her grandmother as Grandma.

Later that day, the minister, his wife, and their two small children came to visit. It didn't take Angie long to realize the children were going to be a problem. Angie nervously watched as the children picked up and played with anything they wanted without their parents saying a word. While the minister and his wife went into Angie's grandmother's room to visit, they left the children to do as they pleased. Angie rushed to the children, saving whatever they were playing with from getting broken. It was obvious they had no respect for her and had no intentions of doing what she asked.

"Angie!" It was the minister. "Come join us for a word of prayer."

She held her grandmother's left hand while the minister and his wife stood on the other side of the bed. Everyone bowed their head and closed their eyes. He had just begun when a sound of something crashing to the floor and breaking came from the living room. Angie looked at her grandmother; her eyes were wide open. She looked at the minister and his wife; they hadn't flinched. She ran to the living room and found the children laughing while jumping on the sofa, and one of her grandmother's prized possessions on the floor, broken into little pieces.

Angie was picking up the pieces of the delicate ceramic statue when she heard, "Come on, boys, it's time to go." As the minister and his family walked around her and out the door, he said, "Call me if you need anything." She didn't answer.

The next day, four ladies from church came to visit, one at a time, and each stayed only a few minutes. They all came empty handed except one. She brought a package of purchased cookies that her children ate, leaving crumbs all over the house. It seemed to Angie the only purpose of their visit was to say a prayer. When they left, they all said about the same thing, "Call me if you need something," or "Let me know if there's anything I can do." She was pleased to see them leave.

It hurt Angie to witness the lack of compassion shown by the people to whom her grandmother had given so much. The hurt was obvious in her grandmother's eyes as she also realized the same. Angie chose to not mention her feelings.

Saturday, Christmas day, Ruby and Gayle arrived early. They joined Angie in her grandmother's bedroom. The three of them said, and at the same time, "Come on, Grandma. It's time to open your presents."

Angie positioned the walker while Ruby and Gayle helped her out of bed.

The girls had placed Grandma's favorite chair close to the tree, and when she was comfortable, they began finding her gifts and taking them to her. Grandma's gifts were wrapped for easy opening; the use of her right arm and hand had improved considerably and she was able to open them without help. Some were humorous, others were comfortable, and some were memorable. She enjoyed them all.

It was painful for Angie to watch her grandmother's eyes sparkle with excitement each time she opened a present, then see the awkward smile that formed, and hear her struggle to say "Thank you." Angie felt her throat tightening and knew tears were soon to follow. To hide her face from her grandmother, she moved beside her and sat on the arm of her chair. It was difficult for Angie to believe that only two weeks before, her grandmother was sitting in that very chair while they planned Christmas day. She even remembered their conversation. It was about inviting Wayne to dinner. *Wayne! I forgot to tell him about Grandma. I wonder if anyone did? Surely someone from church told him. I'll call him later, just to make sure.*

After the living room was put back in order, Ruby said, "Okay, Grandma, we're going to need some help with the cooking. Do you feel up to it?"

She nodded, smiled her little half smile, and struggled to say yes.

They helped her to her feet and to her walker, then walked close to her side as she made her way to the kitchen table. Angie had placed a pen and notepad on the table, and with a face full of joy and a little smile, Grandma held them up to show she was ready.

"Let the fun begin," Ruby shouted.

The day was filled with laughter and happiness as the girls learned from Grandma. But no one enjoyed the day more than Grandma.

It was close to four o'clock by the time they finished eating and the dishes and kitchen were cleaned. Dinner was excellent and they had eaten way too much, which left little room for dessert. They were anxious to try the pies they had baked but were going to have to wait for their stomachs to create some room. They were sitting in the living room reminiscing, laughing, and joking about the day's activities when the phone rang.

"Merry Christmas, Angie. This is Wayne."

She answered loud enough for everyone to hear, "Merry Christmas to you, Wayne. How have you been?"

"I've been doing good. How have you and your grandmother been doing?"

"We had an excellent Christmas, and she's getting better each day."

"What do you mean, 'she's getting better?'"

"You haven't heard? I felt certain someone at church would've told you."

"I haven't been to that church in months. I dislike that dumb minister, and except for your grandmother, the congregation is nothing but a bunch of snobs. But what about your grandmother?"

"She had a stroke."

"Oh my god! I'm so sorry. How is she?"

"She lost some of the use of her right arm and leg, but they're improving and she can get around with the use of a walker. Her speech is affected, so she writes what she wants to say. It's a good thing she's left handed."

"I hear talking in the background. I guess you have several people from her church over?"

"Are you kidding! We haven't heard from or seen anyone from church all day. That's Ruby, Gayle, and Grandma. We finished eating a little while ago, and we're waiting for our food to digest so we can taste the pies that Grandma, Ruby, Gayle, and I baked. How about coming over and joining us for some pie and ice cream?"

"I'd love to. I'll be right there."

Angie

The next day, Wayne, Ruby, and Gayle joined Angie and her grandmother for leftovers. Again, the day ended with no one from church calling or visiting. When all had left and Angie and Grandma were alone, Grandma picked up her pencil and wrote:

I think we should find a new church.

Angie was sitting on the arm of Grandma's chair. She kissed the top of her head. "I agree."

By the middle of the week, Angie realized that she couldn't leave her grandmother alone while attending school. She had to find some help, and if she couldn't find help, there was nothing left to do but drop out of school. When she told her grandmother that she may have to stop going to school for a while, her grandmother wrote:

No! No! No!

Absolutely no!

"What can we do?"

I can take care of myself. I'm sure I can.

"We'll see how the rest of the week goes."

That evening, Wayne came to visit, as he had every day since Christmas. Angie told him of her predicament and asked if he knew someone that did that kind of work. If not, and even though it was against her grandmother's wishes, she would put off school for a while.

Wayne frowned as he listened. "I agree with Maxine. Dropping out of school is not an option, especially in your senior year and with only five months left. If you did, you may not return, and you don't want your grandmother to think that she's responsible for you not graduating. So get that thought out of your head and don't ever let it return. I'll see if I can come up with someone. If not, I'll stay with her. Now I don't want to hear another word about you dropping out of school. Okay?"

"Okay." She went to him, and they hugged. With much effort, she managed to say, "You've been a good friend to both Grandma and me, and we appreciate all you've done."

"I feel the same. Now let's go see how Grandma's doing."

Wayne found an agency that provided people to stay with the disabled. The fee was high, but Angie and her grandmother had no choice. They had to try. Complicating their ability to pay the agency was the large doctor and hospital bills that began arriving. Her grandmother's insurance paid all but 20 percent, but the balance was quite high. Angie wanted to make monthly installments, but her grandmother insisted on paying them off, which left them with very little money. By the time the last medical bill was paid, Maxine's savings account was depleted, and there was only a little more than one thousand in checking.

Two times, Angie had taken money out of her savings to pay the agency; there wasn't much left. She showed her grandmother the balances.

"What are we going to do?"

Don't worry. God will provide.

Two more weeks went by and Angie had to go into her savings again. Where in the past her grandmother had not seemed to worry, she was starting to show concern.

Her grandmother suggested they sell her car. Angie placed an ad in the paper. The car was old, and the best Angie could get was $1,000. The money would not go far. Her grandmother realized they had to do something.

Call my sister in Texas.

She's always wanted to live in Florida.

Maybe she'll come live with us and take care of me.

Angie had called Sally, her grandmother's sister, two days after the stroke and informed her of her grandmother's condition. She had not heard from her since. Angie was reluctant to call, but her grandmother insisted. She was surprised when Sally enthusiastically accepted her invitation.

It was early Sunday afternoon and Angie was mowing. She wanted the yard to look good for Sally when she arrived later in the day. A car pulled in the driveway. She cringed—it was her grandmother's minister. A feeling of relief went through her when she realized his wife and children were not with him. *At least I won't have to stop mowing and watch his brat kids.* He waved as he walked toward the house. She returned his wave and continued mowing.

When she saw the minister walking from the house, toward her, she turned the mower off, then dried her face and eyes with the towel that was draped around her neck. It was an extremely hot day and her clothes were wet with perspiration.

"You know you shouldn't be mowing on the Sabbath" were his first words.

"Good afternoon to you too."

"I haven't seen you in church since your grandmother's stroke."

"No, you haven't."

"Why is that?"

I wonder how Ruby would answer this character? "My grandmother has busted her ass taking care of the sick members of your church, and not one has offered to help her. Sure they all say, 'If you need something, give us a call.' My grandmother never waited for a call: She saw a need and responded. She prepared their food, then took it to them, and not just once, but every day until they were well. She cleaned their house, changed their sheets, washed their clothes, got their prescriptions filled, went to the store if they needed something, and most of the time paid for it with her own money. There have been many nights I woke to hear her in the kitchen baking pies, cakes, and cookies for your dumb bake sales."

"You know your grandmother enjoyed doing the Lord's work."

"Yes, I do. But is she the only one in your congregation that feels a responsibility to care for someone in need?"

"She's in our prayers. I understand that several members came here and prayed for her."

"Big deal. And while they're praying for her, they're letting their kids run wild. And I have to say, your kids are the worst. It takes me a good hour to get the house back in order after one of those praying sessions."

"I'm sorry you feel this way. You know the congregation and I are here to help when you need us."

"I don't see you trying to take this lawnmower away from me and finish mowing."

"I would never mow on a Sunday."

"I'll stop mowing, and you can finish it one day next week. How about that?"

"I'm a busy man with a full week of doing the Lord's work."

"How about someone else in your church?"

"I'll ask."

"Sure, you will. The grass will be up to my ass if I wait on someone from your lazy, inconsiderate congregation to mow it."

"There's no need for that kind of language. I can see that since you've been missing church, you are beginning to stray. I'm going in and tell your grandmother that you should start attending church and stop associating with whoever is influencing your behavior. Your grandmother will not be pleased when I tell her about the lack of respect you've shown me and the vulgar language I've been subjected to."

"You have a one-track mind and haven't understood anything I've said! When you take a collection to buy back my grandmother's car she had to sell to pay the nurse that comes in to care for her so I can go to school. When your members take turns watching her while I'm in school, so we don't have to have a nurse. When someone comes in at night to care for her, so I can go back to work to make enough money to pay for the expensive prescriptions. Or better yet, I'll stay with her at night and the church pay for her prescriptions. And, yes, someone mows this damn grass. That's when I'll return to your dumb church. And not a day before!

"So unless you can guarantee those things will happen, I'd appreciate it if you'd get in your brand-new, expensive car, that was bought for you with some of my grandmother's donations, and leave—and never return."

Angie

He placed his hand on his hips, turned his nose up, and said, "Well, I never."

As she watched him strut away, Ruby's influence surfaced again. "I can't believe you fathered your children!"

CHAPTER 10

The cigarette dangling from the corner of Sally's mouth was the first thing Angie and her grandmother saw—Maxine had forgotten her sister smoked. It had been more than ten years since she last saw her.

From their large living room window, Angie and her grandmother watched as Sally struggled to turn into their driveway. Her steering wheel looked too close to her body, and in an effort to keep the smoke away from her face, her cigarette was in the far right corner of her mouth; she had her head cocked to the left, her right eye closed, and her mouth twisted as far to the right as she could get it; the left side was open and in an awkward location— the middle. Even with all her facial contortions, the smoke was still affecting her eyes.

After helping her grandmother to her walker, Angie went out to greet her aunt. As she walked toward the car, she couldn't help but notice how much larger Sally was than she had imagined.

Angie opened Sally's door, then watched as she twisted around, put both feet on the ground, then struggled to stand. Her legs were extremely short, and from the stain on her large belly, where the steering wheel rubbed, Angie realized why she looked so awkward when she turned in the driveway. The next thing that caught Angie's eye was her oily hair. It was clinging to her head and looked as if it had not been washed in a month. She also observed the crude way Sally dropped her freshly lit cigarette to the ground without putting it out.

"Hi, Sally. I'm Angie." Angie had planned to address her as "Aunt Sally," but after seeing her, "Sally" seemed more appropriate.

"Hi, Angie." They hugged as Sally pulled her dress out of the crack of her behind. She pointed to a suitcase. "That bag and my purse will be all I need for a while. You can get the rest later, when it gets a little cooler."

While carrying Sally's suitcase and following close behind, Angie couldn't help but smile as she watched the movement of Sally's large hips waddle to the house.

To greet her sister, Angie's grandmother, with the help of her walker, was standing just inside the door.

Even before they hugged, Sally said, "Damn, Maxine! You look like you've been hit by a truck!"

Angie grimaced. *That's the last thing Grandma needed to hear.*

Sally went straight for Maxine's favorite chair, plopped her big ass down, and asked, "Where's an ashtray?"

"We don't have one," Angie answered.

"I'm not surprised. I figured that since Maxine doesn't smoke, there might not be one, so I brought my own." She looked toward Angie, then pointed to her suitcase. "It's in my bag. Will you get it for me?" As if Maxine were not in the room, she said, "I imagine your grandmother had rather I didn't smoke in her house, but I came to help, and if I'm going to help, she's going to have to put up with a little smoke."

Angie glanced at her grandmother; she shrugged her left shoulder, then motioned for Angie to get the ashtray. Sally lit a cigarette, then dropped the match in the ashtray as Angie handed it to her. Soon, the room was filled with smoke, and the smell became extremely undesirable. It was as if her grandmother's innocent home had lost something very special. Angie's nose and eyes began to burn, and she knew her grandmother was just as uncomfortable. She couldn't understand why the smoke at work didn't seem to bother her as much. *But,* she thought, *that is work. This is home.*

Angie didn't feel the least bit inconsiderate when she said, "I guess Grandma and I will have to leave our bedroom doors closed."

"I guess you will."

Bruce Collier

Angie never heard such sounds of agony as Sally struggled to get out of her grandmother's chair. Finally, with no help from Angie, she stood.

"Where's the bathroom?"

Angie pointed. "Down the hall."

The room fell silent. Angie looked at her grandmother sitting on the opposite end of the sofa from her and thought how uncomfortable and awkward she looked sitting in a location she was not accustomed with. She whispered, "While Sally's in the bathroom, let's get you back in your chair." She moved closer when she noticed her grandmother writing.

I'm OK. I can stand easier from the sofa.

Angie felt certain her grandmother had rather not give up her comfortable lounge chair, but she realized that, like the house, the chair had been violated, and now that it was tainted, her grandmother would have a difficult time sitting in it. The end of the sofa would be her place to sit.

Angie leaned closer to her grandmother to see what she had written.

I think I've made a big mistake!

"Maybe. And maybe not." Angie knew she had but didn't want to agree and upset her.

Sally returned, sat in her chair, and lit a cigarette. "What do you have to eat?"

Angie looked toward the kitchen. "I'm baking a ham for dinner, but it won't be ready for another two hours."

"I mean something to snack on. Like ice cream, cookies, potato chips, things like that."

"We don't normally eat between meals, so we don't have much to snack on."

"I should've known. I better make a grocery list. Get me a pen and something to write on." With much effort, she stood and waddled into the kitchen. After looking in the refrigerator and pantry, she sat at the table and started the list. "While I'm making this list, you can get the rest of my things out of my car. Then move it so you can get out and go to the grocery store."

94

Angie

Sally had been there for less than an hour, and already, Angie was tired of being bossed around. "I'll get your stuff out of your car, but I'll go to the store after school tomorrow. I've been mowing and I need a shower. I also have to prepare dinner."

"I can't wait until you get home from school. I'm used to having a little snack between meals. You don't even have any Coke or Pepsi. I can't imagine starting the day without one."

"I'll go after dinner."

When Angie returned from her shower, she said, "It'll be a while before dinner, so if you'd like to take a shower?"

"I'm okay. I'll just sit here and talk to Maxine."

Angie couldn't believe Sally wasn't going to take a shower. She also noticed that she said "talk to" not "talk with." And she didn't offer to help with dinner. *What a lazy, inconsiderate bitch. This is not going to be fun.*

When dinner was ready, Angie helped her grandmother stand and, with the help of her walker, walk to the kitchen.

Sally had the lounge chair in the reclining position, watching TV. "Would you mind fixing me a plate? I'll eat in here. I like to watch TV while eating, and I can't see it from the kitchen."

Angie looked at her grandmother shaking her head. "I'm sorry, but Grandma won't allow eating in the living room."

"Jesus! I can't believe she has such silly rules." She put out her cigarette, struggled to stand, and still managed to be first at the dinner table. Angie turned the TV off.

Sally was getting comfortable when Angie said, "That's Grandma's place. She sits at the head of the table and I sit here, beside her."

"My god! You even have special places to sit."

"Yes, we do."

Sally's plate was across from Angie. And after a few minutes of watching Sally eat, she wished she had let her eat in the living room—she felt sure her grandmother wished the same. Both arms were spread across the table, and while holding her tea in one hand and holding her fork like a shovel in the other, she shoveled her food in her mouth as fast as she could swallow. Actually, her face was so close to her plate, it looked more like she was raking the food in rather than shoveling. Even though Maxine's mouth was partially paralyzed, she had less food on her face than Sally. Sally devoured her food without saying a word and was finished long before Angie and her grandmother.

Angie kept her eye on the pack of cigarettes beside Sally's plate. She had made up her mind that she was not going to let her light one at the table. And just as she suspected, Sally reached for her cigarettes as soon as she swallowed her last bite.

Angie's insides were shaking with tension; she didn't want to say anything but knew she had to. "Please don't light one at the table."

"Why not?"

"Why not!" She had lost control. "The least you can do is be considerate and show a little respect for Grandma, especially while she's trying to eat."

"Well! If that's the way you feel. I'll go watch TV."

While the TV blared, Angie heard her grandmother trying to get her attention; she leaned closer.

"Thank you," her grandmother whispered. It was difficult, but she continued, "I'm sorry."

Angie patted her grandmother's hand. "Don't worry, Grandma. It'll be all right."

When Angie finished washing the dishes and cleaning the kitchen, she looked at the grocery list. She was shocked when she noticed there was nothing on the list but junk food and frozen dinners. *Grandma and I can't eat this crap. Maybe this is all she knows how to cook? And since she'll be doing the cooking, I better get what she asked for.*

Angie

Sally was still in bed and Angie was cleaning the breakfast dishes; her grandmother was writing:

Now that Sally is here, why don't you start back to work?

"Are you sure?"

She nodded.

"I have several things to do after school today, but I'll make time to stop by the restaurant and talk with them. And if it's okay with them and you're sure you'll be all right, I'll go back to work."

I'll be fine.

⸎

It was close to six o'clock by the time Angie arrived home. The house was filled with smoke, her grandmother was sitting on the sofa, and Sally was laid back in the lounge chair watching TV. Seeing her grandmother in an awkward position on the sofa while Sally enjoyed the comfort of the lounge chair was almost more than Angie could bear. She fought back tears and hugged her grandmother. Neither said a word; they didn't need to. Her grandmother's eyes said it all; the day had not gone well.

She looked toward Sally and asked in a loud enough voice to be heard over the blaring TV, "What's for dinner?"

Without looking at Angie, she said, "I've been so occupied in this program that I haven't even thought about dinner. How about putting each of us a couple of those pot pies in the oven."

Angie looked down at the small table Sally had moved next to her chair; it and the floor around it were cluttered with cigarette ashes, candy wrappers, chip bags, and empty Coke bottles. *That lazy bitch! Not only does Grandma have to endure the smoke in her once clean house, which now smells like an ashtray, but has to watch as it is strewn from one end to the other with crumbs and trash.*

⸎

After a trying dinner of chicken pot pies (Grandma and Angie each had one; Sally had two), Angie's grandmother headed for her bedroom. Angie joined her when she finished cleaning the kitchen.

Her grandmother was in her bed, holding her pad and pencil. After closing the door, Angie sat beside her and read what she had written:

This is not working.

I don't know what to do.

"You're right. It's not working. We have to take charge. Give me a few days to come up with something. I've decided to wait until next week before starting back to work, but if things haven't improved by then, I'll wait a little longer.

"It hurts me to see you suffering with her smelly cigarette smoke. And that's the first thing I'll stop. You will back me with my decisions, won't you?"

She nodded.

"Your disability check should start arriving soon, and with me working, we should be able to make it. Besides, the way you're improving, we may not need any help."

There was a knock on the door at the same time it began to open. Grandma put the notepad face down against her chest.

"I forgot to mention," Sally said, "a man named Wayne called. He said he's bringing spaghetti over for dinner tomorrow night. He also said to call him if you have other plans."

"Oh, boy! We love his spaghetti sauce. Don't we, Grandma?" Without waiting for her grandmother's reply, she turned back to Sally. "He makes the best."

Angie was pleased, but by the concerned look in her grandmother's eyes, it was obvious that she wasn't. When Sally left and the door was closed, Grandma began to write:

I don't want Wayne to see our house looking like this!

"Don't worry. I'll come straight home from school and clean it."

But what about the smoke smell?

"I'll try to hide it with some room deodorizer. Don't worry. Everything will be fine."

After saying hello to Angie, Wayne's next words were "Who in the hell is smoking!"

Sally returned the back of the chair to its up position and put out her cigarette. "That would be me."

Angie took the pot of spaghetti sauce. "Wayne, this is Sally, Grandma's sister."

Wayne glared at Sally for a moment without saying anything or offering his hand. He kissed Maxine on the cheek, then accompanied Angie to the kitchen.

When Sally couldn't see him, he motioned to Angie to join him on the patio. "I'm sorry, Angie, but I can't handle that cigarette smoke, and I don't know how you and your grandmother can either. And I also don't understand why you are."

"We asked her to come stay with us, hoping she would help while I'm in school, but so far, she hasn't been any help. If anything, it's more of a problem with her here. I intend to talk with her when I get a plan together."

"For your grandmother's sake, make it soon. Do you mind if I suggest something?"

"No, not at all. In fact, I'll welcome your suggestions."

"I think you should come up with some rules. With no smoking in the house at the top of the list. If she has to smoke, she can do it out here on the patio. If she packs and leaves, you'll be better off. And remember this, and I truly mean what I'm saying, if Fat Ass does leave, I'll help you."

Angie almost laughed out loud at Wayne's name for Sally. Then, while struggling to regain her composure, she said, "Making rules is a good idea, and I'll make no smoking, except on the patio, number one."

"Maxine doesn't need the added tension, so you'll have to enforce them. Now, where are we going to eat tonight? I damn sure can't eat with all that smoke. As I see it," he continued, "we have two choices: we can eat out here, or you and Maxine can leave Fat Ass here and come with me to my house."

"I think it'll be best if we eat here, on the patio. Grandma won't feel comfortable leaving…Fat Ass."

Wayne chuckled, put his arm around her, and said, "Okay, I'll warm the sauce and start the water boiling for the spaghetti."

"And I'll set the table and put the bread in the oven."

"Dinner's ready, Sally," Angie called into the living room. Wayne had already helped her grandmother to a chair, at the table, on the patio.

Sally was shocked to see the patio table set. "Can't handle the smoke?"

Before Angie could say anything, Wayne said, "You damn right, I can't handle it. And I don't see how Maxine and Angie can handle it either. And I don't understand how you can force them to endure it." He looked at Maxine, then Angie. "I'm sorry. I had no right to say that." He looked back at Sally. "But I do think that's really inconsiderate of you."

"If you don't mind," Sally said, "I'll take my food to the living room."

"I shouldn't have said what I said," Wayne said. "Stay and eat with us."

"That's okay," Angie said. "Most of the time, she eats in the living room."

"She does *what*! Again, I'm sorry." He placed his hand on Maxine's and, when Sally could no longer hear him, said, "You and Angie have to do something about your house guest. All this cigarette smoke and the tension she's causing is definitely something you don't need."

Angie answered for her, "We know." She placed her hand on Grandma's other hand and quietly said, "Wayne has a good idea. He said we should make some rules and stick to them."

"I also said if she leaves, I'll help. I meant what I said, so don't be afraid you'll piss her off and she'll leave. It's my opinion that if she leaves, you'll be better off."

Maxine removed her hand from under his, placed it on his, and patted it.

Wayne felt the need to change the subject. "How about you and Angie joining me this Sunday and going to church?"

"What church?" Angie asked.

"My church."

"For the last several months, Wayne has been attending a different church," Angie said to her grandmother. "I think we should go. Don't you?"

She nodded in agreement and smiled.

"We have a date," Wayne said. "I'll pick you up Sunday morning."

Wayne was helping Angie clean the kitchen and dishes, and when he went into the living room to get Sally's empty plate, he asked, "What did you think of my sauce?"

"It wasn't bad. You gave me way too much. I'm not used to eating that much."

Angie heard what Sally said and knew Wayne was holding back from saying, "You look like you don't eat much."

When it was time for Wayne to leave and Angie was seeing him to the door, he said, "I'll see you and your grandmother Sunday morning." He left without saying anything to Sally.

When he could no longer hear her, Sally asked, "Why is he coming back Sunday?"

"He's taking Grandma and me to church."

"I don't like that man!"

"That's too bad. He's a good friend, and you'll be seeing a lot of him."

CHAPTER 11

Angie's grandmother motioned to her and Sally that she was going to bed. Angie said she would be in to see her as soon as she finished cleaning the kitchen. It was a little early for Grandma to be going to bed, but Angie figured she was anxious to be in her room, with the door closed, and out of the cigarette smoke. Getting away from Sally was probably another reason. Angie felt certain her grandmother was also having a difficult time dealing with the embarrassment she suffered when Wayne found her house full of cigarette smoke and the stress caused by Sally's sarcastic remarks.

Angie closed the door behind her and sat on the side of the bed. Her grandmother handed her a note:

> I can't go through another day like the last two have been, or a night like tonight. You have no idea how bad the cigarette smoke is during the day.
>
> Watching her sit in that chair all day, smoking and eating is about to drive me crazy.
>
> I know I told you I'll back you with whatever decision you make, but I'm the one responsible for her being here and I should be the one who straightens her out.
>
> I wish I knew what to say or what to do.

If I upset her, she'll leave and then we're back where we started. But in all honesty, I'd rather be alone than deal with the stress of her being here.

I know you'd worry, but I'm sure I can take care of myself.

This is our home. We need to get it back.

Angie tore the note from the pad. She had saved all her grandmother's notes; this one would join the others.

"You did what you thought was a good idea, but you had no reason to believe she was this inconsiderate. I also thought it was the perfect answer. She'd be in Florida, as she always wanted, and you'd have some help. But unfortunately, that's not the way it is. We have a predicament that we'll just have to solve. As Wayne suggested, let's make some rules. Number one rule: there will be no more smoking in the house, except out on the patio. What's next?"

No more eating in the living room.

"Good one. Only let's make it: no eating anyplace except in the kitchen. What else?"

Dinner no later than seven o'clock.

"Another good one. I think that's enough for now. Let's see how she adapts to these. I'd rather tell her tomorrow when I get home from school, if you can stand the smoke until then?"

I can. That'll give you more time to prepare.

I know it'll be difficult for you, but I want you to know, I'll back you.

I'm just sorry you have to go through this.

You would think she would have enough sense to see the discomfort she's causing and be agreeable, but she won't.

So let's agree to be strong and stand by our decisions!

"I agree." Angie paused a moment before continuing. "You know? It's amazing how similar Mom was to Sally: inconsiderate, demanding, the same arrogant personality. And just like Mom, she seems to be allergic to soap and water. She hasn't had a shower or bath since she's been here, has she?"

Her grandmother shook her head.

⁓

Angie had struggled all day with how to start her conversation with Sally. When the time was right, she was ready.

"Sally, Grandma and I have decided that we had rather you not smoke in the house."

"You have, have you?"

"Yes."

"Why? Just because your friend can't handle the smoke?"

"No. But it is unfortunate that our friends have to be subjected to it. The reason is Grandma and I can't handle it. We appreciate you being here and we've tried to tolerate the smoke, but we can't. We hope you understand."

"Well, I'm not going to stop smoking, so it looks to me like you have a problem."

"Whether you quit or not is not our problem, it's yours, but if you have to smoke, you can smoke on the patio, not in the house."

"On the patio! I'm not going to go out there to smoke. There's no TV or decent chair to sit in. I might as well go home!"

"I'm sorry you feel that way, but you're not going to smoke in the house." She wanted to say, "Don't let the door hit your fat ass."

"I'll try it for a few days, but if I'm not comfortable with it, I'm out of here!"

Angie felt it would be best to hold off on telling her the rest of what she planned to say.

⁓

The next three days were tense for Angie and her grandmother, and the house still had the strong smell of smoke. Sally didn't smoke in the living room when they were with her, but they suspected she did after they went to bed. They also figured she smoked in her bedroom and in the bathroom. Every time Sally went out to the patio, she made a comment about how ridiculous she thought it was. When Angie showed compassion for her suffering, she was rewarded with a sarcastic remark. Sally seemed to enjoy keeping them tense and uncomfortable.

Before Sally, Angie had never looked forward to attending church; now she was eagerly waiting for Sunday.

When Wayne arrived, Angie and her grandmother were ready and waiting. Sally was still sleeping.

Wayne introduced them to several people as they entered the church, and by the gracious way they were welcomed, it was obvious that this was a much different church than the one they were accustomed to. There was a noticeable difference in respect, sincere interest, and compassion shown to Angie and her grandmother. These people were nothing like the snobbish, pretentious people at the other church. A man, who was just introduced to Maxine, held her walker while Angie and Wayne helped her up the steps where the minister was waiting to greet her. Angie stepped back while the minister hugged and welcomed her, then he and Wayne escorted her in and to a nice pew up front. Angie could barely hold back her tears.

"I wonder where Sally is?" Angie said when she noticed Sally's car wasn't in the driveway.

"She probably went to get something to eat," Wayne answered, "or more cigarettes."

After helping Wayne with getting her grandmother in, Angie looked in Sally's bedroom.

"She's gone! She's gone! Hallelujah, she's gone!" Angie could tell by the little half-smile and the twinkle in her grandmother's eyes that she was just as pleased. "We have our house back, Grandma."

Wayne helped Maxine to the location on the sofa she had become accustomed to. "You have a seat while Angie and I open the windows. And while your house is airing out, we'll go get some lunch."

On the way back, they bought some air freshener, disinfectant, and a new air conditioner filter. The first thing Wayne did when they returned home was change the filter in the air conditioner and turn it on. Angie closed the windows. Next they cleaned and disinfected Grandma's chair, and while it was drying, they cleaned, disinfected, and deodorized the rest of the house. When Grandma's chair was dry, Wayne held his hand out to her.

"Allow me to help you to your chair. You look out of place and uncomfortable sitting on this sofa."

Wayne chose a chair, slouched back in it with his legs straight out in front, took a sip of the ice-cold tea Angie had brought him, and said, "Now, this is more as it should be. Angie, what's for dinner?"

"I don't know. All we have is a bunch of frozen dinners that Sally had me buy."

"I'm sure you're tired of eating frozen dinners, so let's go out to eat."

"I think Grandma is too tired to go out, so if you don't mind, let's eat frozen dinners."

"Frozen dinners it is. What wine do you suggest?"

Even Grandma laughed.

Before Wayne left, he told them he would return around nine o'clock the next morning. "Don't worry about your grandmother. I'll take good care of her."

"Thank you, Wayne. And thanks for taking Grandma to church, she needed that. You've been a wonderful friend. I don't know how we could've made it without you."

Angie

Angie rushed home after school to relieve Wayne. Her grandmother's face sparkled with excitement as she motioned to Wayne.

Wayne smiled. "She wants me to tell you about our minister dropping by today."

She nodded and smiled.

It had been a long time since Angie had seen her grandmother that excited and happy. Angie gave her grandmother a hug, as she did every day when she returned from school, only this one was longer and with more enthusiasm.

"It looks like he brightened your day."

She nodded.

Wayne stood. "I guess I better be going. Is there anything you need from the store?"

"I can't think of anything. But thanks for asking. Grandma and I really appreciate you staying with her today, but we feel like we're taking advantage of your friendship. We'll talk tonight and figure out how we can manage without imposing on you."

"Don't worry about it. It's taken care of."

"What do you mean?"

"You'll see. I have to go. I'll see you tomorrow."

"Goodbye, and thanks." Angie still heard his words and was curious. "Grandma, do you know what he meant?"

She shook her head and shrugged her shoulder.

Angie was startled by the knock on the door. She wondered who it could be. It was too early for Wayne. She looked out the window and saw a strange car parked along the curb and a woman she didn't recognize standing at their door. Angie cautiously opened the door.

"Can I help you?"

"Hi. Are you Angie?"

"Yes."

"My name is Kelly. I'm here to take care of your grandmother."

"But…"

"Rev. Buchanan sent me."

"But I'm sorry, there must be a mistake. We can't afford to pay you."

"Don't worry. The church pays my fee."

"Oh my god! I can't believe this."

"I'm one of several retired ladies the church pays to care for those who need help. Most of us are retired caregivers in some form or another, and some, like me, are retired nurses. Not only does the service help the shut-ins, it provides us with a little extra money."

"What a church! And what a wonderful man Rev. Buchanan is. Come with me. I'll introduce you and Grandma." She couldn't control her excitement as she ran ahead of Kelly: "Grandma! Guess what? Wayne's church is providing this lady to care for you. Kelly, this is my grandmother, Maxine."

Maxine's right arm was always difficult to move in the mornings, so while still in bed, she raised her left arm.

Kelly gently held her hand and said, "It's nice meeting you, Maxine. I need to talk with Angie before she leaves for school, then I'll be back." As Angie left the room with Kelly, she looked back at her grandmother, and even though her smile was small, her face and eyes expressed her joy.

After showing Kelly where her grandmother's medicine was and discussing her routine, she finished getting ready for school. Kelly returned to her grandmother. Angie could not believe what was happening and was having a difficult time convincing herself. Before leaving for school, and as usual, she kissed her grandmother goodbye, then told Kelly goodbye and thanked her.

Angie rushed straight home from school.

"How'd it go?" Angie asked Kelly as she closed the door behind her.

"We had a great day, but I'll let Maxine tell you about it. I've really enjoyed being with your grandmother. She's a wonderful lady."

She turned toward Maxine. "I have to go now, but I'm looking forward to tomorrow. I'll see you in the morning."

Maxine began writing with enthusiasm as soon as Kelly left.

"I'll put my books in my room and be right back."

Her grandmother anxiously handed her the note.

Kelly is *wonderful!*

I've had a fabulous day.

Two ladies dropped by around noon with something to eat.

After we ate, the ladies stayed and we played cards.

Rev. Buchanan came to visit and joined in our card came.

He's also a wonderful person.

It's something how Wayne and Rev. Buchanan have changed our lives.

Now I look forward to my tomorrows, and I definitely look forward to Sunday.

I'm so happy I could shout. (If I could.)

Will you call Wayne and express my feelings?

"I won't have to. He just drove up."

After saying their hellos, Angie handed him Grandma's note. He read it then said, "I'm so delighted that you're pleased with Kelly and the program our church provides. I wish I could take some of the credit, but I can't. I had no idea the church offered this assistance until yesterday when Rev. Buchanan told me. The difference in our new church and our old one is unbelievable. Especially the ministers."

Angie was quick to say, "You can say that again!"

CHAPTER 12

Angie and her grandmother had looked forward to Sunday and were anxious to get to church and express their appreciation to Rev. Buchanan and others. This time, as Wayne and Angie helped her up the steps, even more people than before came to help and welcome her. It had been many months since Angie had seen her grandmother that happy; it was a welcome change.

The doors of the ambulance were closing as Angie parked by the curb. She rushed to find Kelly.

"What happened!"

"I think your grandmother has suffered another stroke or maybe a heart attack."

"How could that be?" she asked as the ambulance pulled away. "Yesterday, she felt great, especially at church."

"She felt that way today, right up until a few minutes ago. She was sitting in her chair when I heard her make a strange sound. I looked toward her, and she was having trouble breathing. I called the ambulance, then rushed back to her. She continued struggling to breathe until the ambulance arrived and they began giving her oxygen. Never before have I been that glad to see an ambulance arrive."

"Would you call Wayne and ask him to meet me at the hospital? His number is by the phone."

"I'll call him. And good luck."

Angie

Angie rushed to Wayne when she saw him enter the waiting room. They held each other without saying a word, then while continuing their embrace, he asked, "How is she?"

"I don't know. The nurses won't tell me anything nor will they let me see her."

"It's best if we stay out here. We'd just be in their way."

"You're right." She looked toward the restroom sign and said, "I'll be right back."

As before, she held the cold paper towel against her face and eyes until it was warm. She felt a little better when she left the restroom but became concerned when she saw Wayne talking to a man who appeared to be a doctor. His eyes said a lot, but when he opened his arms to her, that told it all—Grandma was gone.

Without saying a word, they held each other and cried. Wayne told the doctor he would get back with him. Then, while holding each other, they walked away.

"How about coming home with me? You shouldn't be alone tonight. Especially, alone in your grandmother's home."

"You're probably right, but I want to go home. If I'm home, I'll feel closer to her and I want to be as close as possible."

"I understand. But I will insist on driving you home. We can get your car tomorrow."

"Okay."

Angie rested her head against the window and softly cried. They were more than halfway home before either spoke. Wayne broke the silence. "I'll call Rev. Buchanan as soon as we get home. We'll let him make the arrangements, if that's all right with you."

She nodded her approval.

Angie silently lay across her bed, reminiscing about her grandmother and wondering what her life was going to be like without her. She also realized there was no way she could be involved in arranging her grandmother's funeral. She was relieved when Wayne told her that Rev. Buchanan was taking care of everything.

"I really don't want to leave you alone and I know Ruby's working, so do you mind if I call Gayle?"

Without looking up, she said, "Her number is in the address book beside the phone."

"Her mother is bringing her over," Wayne said as he sat beside her. "I also called Fat Ass Sally. She said to tell you that you'll be in her prayers, and since she was just here, she won't be coming to the funeral."

"That's a relief."

⁓

"I'm sorry…I'm so sorry" was all Gayle could say as she and Angie hugged and cried. After a few minutes, Gayle said, "I called Ruby at work. She said she'll be here soon. I also brought my clothes for school. Ruby will take me."

Ruby arrived soon after Gayle, and after she and Angie embraced and cried for a while, she and Gayle sat on the edge of the bed with her, one on either side. Each with an arm around her, they listened and comforted her as she explained what happened.

Wayne stood beside them. "I wish I had some intelligent or comforting words to ease the pain, but I don't. It'll just take time."

Angie lifted her eyes to his. "You're right. But it takes a lot longer to get over someone as good as Grandma."

"That's true," Wayne said. "I guess I better be getting home. Angie, what do you think about Ruby going with me and bringing your car back? I hate to leave it overnight in the hospital parking lot."

"That's a good idea. If Ruby doesn't mind."

"I'll be glad to."

⁓

Ruby took Gayle to school, then returned and stayed until she had to leave for home and get ready for work. Wayne and Rev.

Buchanan arrived soon after she left. While discussing the funeral arrangements, Angie mentioned that several months earlier, her grandmother had informed her that when she passed away, she wanted her casket closed at all times and she wanted to be cremated and her ashes spread in the Gulf. Rev. Buchanan said he would arrange everything except spreading her ashes.

Wayne reached for Angie's hand. "Angie and I will take care of that."

"I have scheduled the service for Friday. Will that be all right with you?"

Angie and Wayne agreed.

Wayne stayed until Gayle called and asked if he or Angie could come get her. She was home from school with no way to get there. Angie suggested they both go.

Wayne, Ruby, and Gayle had agreed that one or more of them would stay with Angie through the weekend. Angie told them earlier that she was staying home from school for the rest of the week; she planned to return on Monday. Her grandmother's attorney called on Wednesday and asked if she could come in the next day to go over her grandmother's will.

Wayne accompanied her to the attorney's office. Her grandmother had left Angie her house, her car—that she no longer owned—all her possessions, and a $5,000 insurance policy. Angie's Social Security check that her grandmother received was a direct deposit in her checking account, and since Angie's name was on her grandmother's checking and savings account, getting to those funds and the little money left was not a problem. The attorney said he would notify the insurance company and the check would come to Angie. He suggested that since it was only three months until her eighteenth birthday, they could save a lot of paperwork if they wait until then to put the house in her name. He also said that her grandmother and he had been friends for many years, and he would not be charging a fee.

Wayne escorted Angie, Ruby, and Gayle through the side door of the church and to the area reserved for family; Angie sat between Gayle and Ruby, Wayne sat next to Ruby, on the outside, close to the aisle. Even though Angie's throat was so tight, she could hardly breathe or speak, and her chest felt as if it were about to explode, she held back her tears. But as soon as Rev. Buchanan took the podium and looked at her, she lost control, put her face in her hands and handkerchief, and began to weep. With tears running down their cheeks, Ruby and Gayle put their arms around her and held her close.

Rev. Buchanan gave a very warm, upbeat service. Many of the friends she had cared for from her other church were there, and by Rev. Buchanan's comments, it was obvious that he had talked with them. Angie was amazed at how accurately he portrayed her grandmother's compassion, her generosity, and her sense of humor, especially, when two weeks was all he had known her.

Angie and Ruby were alone. It was Sunday night and Angie was preparing her clothes for school.

"How 'bout moving in with me?" Angie asked. "There's plenty of room. We could share expenses, and I'd love the company. What do you think?"

"I'd love to."

"Good."

"I'll call my parents tonight and tell them. And tomorrow, while you're in school, and before I go to work, I'll move my clothes and things."

The phone was ringing as Angie opened the door; she had just gotten home from school. It was Wayne.

"I picked up Maxine's ashes today, and I was wondering if today is a good day for us to take a boat ride?"

"I'm going to start back to work tomorrow, so today is the perfect day. I'll be right over."

Wayne's boat was docked in the canal behind his house. It was 25' long with a large cockpit, a roomy cabin, and a helm station with a canopy and windshield large enough to give adequate protection from the weather. When Angie arrived, the engine was running, the lines were untied, and Wayne was holding the boat to the dock.

Wayne held Angie's hand and helped her board. They pushed off, and he took up his position behind the helm. Angie was standing beside him as they slowly motored out the canal. When she moved toward the companion seat, she noticed the box. "Is that…?"

"Yes, it is."

She held her grandmother's ashes in her lap with both hands as they proceeded to her grandmother's final resting place. Wayne adjusted the boat's speed to a slow, comfortable pace. He maintained that speed even after leaving Longboat Pass and entering the gulf. It was a beautiful day, the sun was low in the sky, and the clouds were showing a little gold as they prepared for the sunset that was sure to follow. When the boat cleared the bell buoy, Wayne turned north and stopped soon after.

"I think your grandmother would prefer to not be placed far out to sea. Do you agree?"

"Yes."

Wayne let the boat slow to a stop, then turned the ignition off. A few moments before, all Angie heard was the roar of the engine. Now, with the turn of the key, the evening became totally silent. The only sound was a lone seagull circling overhead, hoping that one of them would toss it something to eat.

A light warm breeze was blowing from the west, so they moved to the east side of the boat, the starboard side. Angie was holding her grandmother's ashes tightly against her chest. Her chin was quivering and tears were running down her cheeks.

"Would you like me to do it?" Wayne asked.

She wrapped her arms tighter around the box and shook her head. After a few minutes of silence, she moved closer to the side.

"I've done this before," Wayne said. "You'll need to lean way over and hold the box close to the water, that way the ashes won't blow back in your face."

When the box was close to the water, she removed the lid and poured its contents on the surface of the crystal-clear water. Wayne put his arm around her, and they watched as the ashes slowly sank out of sight.

"Goodbye Grandma. Thanks for all you did for me. I'm going to miss you."

"I'll miss you too, Maxine. Goodbye."

They silently watched the water for several minutes; it was as if they were in a trance. Neither said a word as they returned to their seats. Without looking at Angie, Wayne started the engine, and with the engine barely more than an idle, turned the boat west, in the direction of the sun. The sky was a little hazy, which helped protect their eyes from the sun's bright light as it began to dip below the surface.

"Oh my god," Angie said when the last of the big red ball was swallowed by the gulf. "What a beautiful sunset. And what a beautiful closure to a beautiful lady. It's as if Grandma is telling us goodbye."

"I agree. Let's go home." He turned the boat around, pushed the throttle forward, and in just a few minutes, they were back at his dock.

Angie was still holding the box when she stepped on the dock.

Wayne reached for it. "I'll dispose of that for you. Unless you'd rather keep it?"

She handed him the box. "I'd rather not."

When the boat was secured, Angie put her arms around Wayne and kissed him on the cheek. "Thanks for everything. I don't know how Grandma and I could've made it without you."

With his arm around her, he kissed her forehead. "It was a pleasure being a part of your grandmother's life. I feel honored to have known her. And I'm just as pleased knowing that we are friends. I hope it doesn't end."

"It won't."

"What do you say we end the day by going out to dinner?"

"I'd love to."

CHAPTER 13

Angie returned to work, and it did not take long for her charming personality to return as it was before her grandmother's death. In the beginning, she worried that her fake smile was obvious and a distraction, but after a few days, it was no longer fake. Ruby had settled into her new home with Angie, and except for breakfast and work, they rarely saw each other. Angie always seemed to be rushed. She rushed to get ready for school, rushed to get to work after school, then rushed home to finish her homework. At least, by staying busy, she wasn't thinking about or missing her grandmother.

The insurance policy her grandmother left was barely enough to pay the doctor and hospital bills and the funeral expenses, which left Angie with very little money. She and Ruby had agreed that all expenses, such as food, electricity, water, and phone would be split down the middle.

The weekends that Ruby didn't have to work, she was with her boyfriend. On those days, Angie and Gayle went shopping or to a movie. Gayle didn't have a boyfriend and seldom dated. As usual, only men in their late twenties or early thirties were confident enough to ask Angie for a date. She would thank them for asking, then politely say she was seventeen and still in school. That usually discouraged them.

One Friday night, two young men came in the restaurant. Angie greeted them, "Hi. Two for dinner?"

"Unfortunately," the more aggressive one answered.

"Do you prefer smoking or nonsmoking?"

"Nonsmoking."

"There's about a ten-minute wait for nonsmoking. Will that be okay?"

"How long is the wait for smoking?"

"I can seat you now."

The shy one shook his head. "We'll wait."

"If you like, you can have a drink at the bar. I'll come get you when your table is ready."

"I could go for a drink," the aggressive one said, "but I'm afraid we're not old enough. We'll wait out here."

"I'll call you. What name should I use?"

"Rod!" the aggressive one answered. "As in 'hot rod.'"

The shy one put his head down, turned, and walked away.

They sat not far from Angie while waiting. Angie could not help but notice that each time she looked toward them, Rod was talking and the other fellow was looking at her. His eyes always dropped as soon as they made eye contact. He was checking her out, and she was just as interested in checking him out. She had already observed that he was an inch or two taller than Rod and three to four inches taller than she. Earlier, when they walked in, she had admired his broad, straight shoulders and his long muscular arms. Even though he was dressed casually with his shirt out, she could tell his waist and hips were small. She wasn't sure if his bronze skin was natural or the results of a perfect tan, but no matter which, his light brown eyes were enhanced by its color. She found it difficult to keep her eyes from drifting toward his.

It was well over a year when she last felt what she was feeling. His casual glances stirred up desires that she had controlled and suppressed.

Angie was noticeably nervous as she escorted them to their table. She handed them their menus and told them about the specials, then without hesitating, said, "I'm Angie. I know Hot Rod's name, what's yours?"

"Skip."

A warm current flowed through her as her eyes fixed on his smile and eyes.

⌒〜〜

For the first time in many months, Angie was finding it difficult to concentrate on her homework. Her thoughts were about Skip. The look on his face when she asked his name was etched in her memory; she could still see his small shy smile, his beautiful eyes, and hear his voice when he answered. Her thoughts kept returning to their casual glances and the feelings they generated. She wondered if he experienced the same tingling sensation.

Out of all the guys she had seen in the restaurant, she wondered why Skip was the only one who had intrigued her. Was his perfect body the reason? His good looks? Or was it a combination of both? There had been many with those same features, but like Rod, they were stuck on themselves. Most fellows she made casual eye contact with would start flirting and try to impress her with their bragging. Finally, it dawned on her—it was his reserved personality that attracted her. It was as if he preferred her to make the first move. She felt she had by making and holding eye contact while asking his name. She told herself that if she ever saw him again, she would make sure he knew she was interested.

⌒〜〜

Angie was looking at the names on her list of reservations when she heard a soft voice.

"Hi, Angie."

She looked up. It was Skip.

A smile instantly burst into bloom; she felt her face express her pleasure.

"Hi, Skip."

"Hi," he said again.

"No Hot Rod tonight?"

"I'm alone."

It was late in the evening, and most of the customers had left. As she escorted him into the dining room, she said, "I have the perfect table for you." She walked beside him as she directed him to a booth in a secluded area. "Will this be okay?"

"Perfect."

The menu was trembling as she handed it to him, and she had trouble remembering the specials. She wasn't going to walk away without saying something. "I was hoping you'd return."

He looked up from his menu. "It was a long weekend."

"I'll be back a little later and talk with you." Her body, but mostly her insides, shook with excitement as she walked back to the podium.

Angie had seated Skip at one of the tables Ruby was serving. Angie motioned to Ruby and, with her lips only, said, "That's Skip."

When Ruby finished taking his drink order, she returned to Angie. With her eyes all dreamy looking and pretending to fan herself with her hand, she said, "What a hunk."

"I told you."

"I wonder why he's alone?"

"I'm pretty sure he came to see me."

"Hot damn! I'll find out."

"Please don't embarrass him…or me."

"I won't. I'll be really careful." She looked back as she walked away. "Trust me."

A few minutes later, Angie looked up and saw Ruby walking toward her, smiling. "I didn't have to say a word. He began asking questions about you as soon as I returned to take his order."

"What kind of questions?"

"His first question was are you dating someone."

"You're kidding!"

"No, I'm not! Then he asked how old you are, and are you still going to school."

Angie had to hold back the "Yes!" that was about to explode from her, but there was no way she could control her large expressive smile.

"Will it be all right if I tell him I live with you?" Ruby asked. "I don't want him to find out later and think I deceived him."

"Yes. I agree. That'll be best."

"Can I also tell him that you mentioned him to me?"

"Ruby!"

"It's a quick way to break the ice and get something started."

"Oh god! How embarrassing. But you're right. I might as well let my interest be known."

"Good. I'll be right back."

When Ruby returned, her smile was large. "He's not dating anyone. He's nineteen. He graduated last year. He would like to get to know you. And I think he's a super guy. Did I do good?"

Angie could barely control her desire to squeal. "You did great!"

While holding her arms out, Ruby said, "Well?"

Angie wrapped her arms around Ruby, and while they embraced, she said, "Tell him I'll drop by and talk with him when a few more customers leave."

"I'll tell him, but you better hurry before I put a move on him."

"You wouldn't?"

"You know I wouldn't. But as good-looking as he is, one of the other waitresses might."

"I'll hurry."

Skip was just finishing his dinner when Angie joined him. She slid into the seat opposite his.

"Hello."

"Hi."

"Thanks to Ruby, I guess there's not much we don't know about each other."

"Not much."

"Are you from here?"

"Yes."

"Sarasota or Bradenton?"

"Sarasota."

Angie was getting uncomfortable with his one- or two-word answers. "Don't you want to know more about me?"

"Yes."

She paused. "What?"

"I realize I'm not much of a talker, but I'd really like to spend some time with you and get to know you better, preferably away from here."

"I'd also like to get to know you."

"Do you have to work every night this week?"

"Yes. Every night plus the weekend."

"How late do you work?"

"Until nine, which was about ten minutes ago."

"Is there any chance of seeing you after work?"

"Not tonight. I have a lot of important homework to do."

"How about tomorrow night?"

"I don't know. What can we do after nine?"

"Drive around, walk on the beach, but mostly talk."

"I can't be out late. I'm still going to school."

"I know. I promise I won't keep you out late."

Angie looked in his eyes before answering; they were sincere. "Okay."

"Tomorrow night?"

"Only if I can bring Ruby and her boyfriend."

"I understand."

"You'll like them."

"I already like Ruby, and I'm sure I'll like her boyfriend."

"We have a date."

"Yes, we do."

Angie left the restaurant soon after Skip. He was unlocking his car.

"Nice car," she said as she walked by.

"Thanks. But it's not mine. It's my brother's."

"Oh. Would you prefer we take my car tomorrow night?"

"My brother is out of town until Friday. He told me I could use it. But thanks for asking."

"See you tomorrow."

"Nine o'clock?"

"Right."

Angie looked up from her work and saw Skip walking toward the restaurant. She glanced at the clock: 8:45. His loose-fitting shirt was not tucked into his jeans, and he was wearing boat shoes without socks. *Ruby is right. He is a hunk.*

Angie sensed that her face was blushing, expressing her joy.

"Hi, Skip."

"Hi, Angie."

His half smile, his warm eyes, and his soft voice caused Angie to search for something to say. "You're early."

"A little."

"Ruby's boyfriend has to work late, so I guess it's just you and me."

"That's too bad. I was looking forward to meeting him."

She smiled. "I doubt that."

"Maybe I wasn't anxious to meet him, but I do want you to be comfortable. If you had rather put it off until tomorrow night or some other night, I'll understand. I'll be disappointed, but I'll understand."

Their eyes were fixed on each other's for a few moments before she answered, "I trust you."

"There's no reason not to."

As they walked to his brother's car, Angie asked, "Where're we going?"

"I was hoping to walk on the beach, but I think it's too cool for that."

"Let's give it a try."

A cool breeze was blowing off the Gulf, and Skip was right, it was a little cool. The water was cold on their bare feet as they walked through the waves that rolled up the beach. The cloudless sky was clear and the twinkling stars looked close enough to touch, and a half moon was just coming up; it was bright, but not so bright that it affected the glitter of the stars. The white sand looked even whiter from the rays of the moon, and the waves breaking, then rushing up the beach, also glistened from the moon's light.

Angie and Skip were walking side by side. Angie was aware of Skip gradually getting closer; their hands touched, and to encourage him, she opened hers. When their palms came together, she eagerly pulled her fingers up between his.

Skip pointed to the North Star and explained how to find it from certain stars in the Big Dipper. She admired his knowledge of the universe.

"You seem to know a lot about the stars."

"Not as much as I'd like to. I took an astronomy class at the Bishop Planetarium, but that just whet my appetite. Maybe someday, when I have time, I'll take some more classes."

A sudden gust of cool wind hit them, and even though Angie had on slacks and a warm shirt, she felt cold.

"I'm beginning to feel cold. I think we should head back to the car."

They turned around, but instead of holding her hand, he put his arm around her. She put her arm around his waist, and they pulled each other close. She looked up at him, hoping he would kiss her, but he didn't. While still looking at him, she asked, "You don't have time now?"

"Time for what?"

"To take more classes."

"Oh. Not really."

"Why not?"

"I've done some dumb things in my life, but last week, I did the dumbest. It seemed like a good idea at the time, but now I regret doing it more than you can imagine."

"What did you do?"

He opened the car door for her without answering. Angie curiously watched as he walked around the car, got in, held the steering wheel with both hands, looked out the windshield, and stared at the beach. The suspense was eating at her, but she patiently waited.

"I've had a rough life, Angie. I'd like to be able to talk about it, but not now. Maybe someday. I will tell you this much. Two weeks ago, my mother passed away, and last week, I joined the navy."

She lifted his right hand from the wheel with both hers and held it in her lap.

"I'm so sorry. I'm sure you miss her."

"Not really. I regret joining the navy more than I miss her. She was a real bitch."

"You're not serious!"

"I wish I wasn't. She caused my brother and me to have a miserable childhood."

"I understand. I had a mother that was less than desirable. She passed away four years ago, and not once have I missed her." She laid her head on his shoulder. "Why do you regret joining the navy?"

He put his arm around her, and she cuddled closer to him. "After the funeral, I had no money and no place to live. I could've moved in with my brother and his new wife, but I didn't want to be a burden. I'm staying with them until Sunday. That's when I leave."

She pulled away. "Oh no! You can't leave Sunday!" She looked into his sad eyes. "Tell me you're kidding."

"I was hoping you'd say something like that."

"That was a test? Right? You're really not leaving?"

"If it was a test, I'd be pleased with the results, but unfortunately, it wasn't. Even though I barely know you, I know I'll miss you. And I haven't even kissed you."

She lifted her face to his and whispered, "What do you say we take care of that?"

They embraced. She felt his lips slowly pressing hers; they matched perfectly. A kiss that started as a gentle kiss soon became a passionate kiss—a kiss she would keep forever. She was trembling as she buried her face against his chest and shoulder. She caressed him and kissed him again when she heard him say he didn't want to go.

She pulled back enough to see his face. "And I don't want you to go."

For several minutes, they held each other without talking.

Angie

Why am I so aggressive? I'm behaving as if I'm starving for affection, which I am, but I shouldn't let it be so obvious. Get control of yourself, and start acting like the person you are.

"I wish I could stay longer," Angie said, "but it's getting late and I better be getting home."

They kissed again.

"Do you have plans for tomorrow night?" he asked while starting the car.

"Yes, I do." Then kissed him on the cheek. "I plan to be with you."

"I like that plan."

Skip drove to the back of the restaurant where Angie's car was parked. "Wow! Is this your '66 Mustang?"

"It's mine. You like it?"

"She's a beauty. By the way it shines, you must polish it quite often and give it a lot of TLC."

"I try." She unlocked her door, then turned and kissed him lightly on the lips. "Same time. Same place."

"Looking forward to tomorrow."

"Me too."

127

CHAPTER 14

"Wake up, wake up, I want to hear all about your date." Ruby was sitting on the side of Angie's bed, shaking her.

Angie had been awake for some time but didn't want to open her eyes and break the image of being back in Skip's arms with his soft lips pressing hers. She was reliving their first kiss and how she had encouraged him, how his shy tongue had pulled away from hers until it was comfortable, and how nervous he was.

She stretched and smiled, then looked at Ruby. "What're you doing up so early?"

"I couldn't sleep. I have to know how your night went."

"It was terrific!"

"Hot damn! When do you see him again?"

"Tonight."

"Sounds serious to me."

"I'm not sure."

"Why? Does his kisses turn you off?"

"Oh, god, no! His kisses are wonderful. They're the best."

Ruby smiled. "How does he compare to the fellow we shared?"

"Much, much better. I've never been turned on like I was last night."

Ruby thought for a moment. "Come to think of it, Bob didn't kiss worth a damn, did he?"

"Now that I have someone to compare him to, you're right, he wasn't worth a damn."

"If you were so turned on and impressed with him, why are you afraid to get serious?"

"I'm not afraid to get serious. I'd like that very much."

Ruby saw Angie's expression change. "What's wrong?"

"Like everything else in my life, he's only temporary."

"How do you know?"

"He's leaving Sunday. He joined the navy."

"Bummer."

"He said he wished he hadn't joined, now that he met me, and I feel certain he's being honest. I can't believe he feels the way he does after only one date."

"It seems to me that you feel the same."

Angie paused for a moment. "I do. I really do. Maybe it's because neither of us have dated much."

"A guy with his looks and body hasn't dated much? That's hard to believe."

"You have no idea how shy and awkward he is. I bet he's never felt a breast or had his hand in a girl's panties."

"You really think he's a virgin?"

"Yes, I do."

"Hot damn! You get to break him in."

"Oh, I don't plan to have sex with him."

"Yeah, right!"

"I'm not. Especially knowing he's leaving Sunday. He thinks his first leave is in eight weeks, but until then, he'll write. Eight weeks isn't so long."

"I agree. You should wait."

"It's getting late. I better get ready for school."

Angie was ready and anxious when Skip arrived at the restaurant. They walked on the beach like the night before, only this time they held each other close. Their conversation was basically the same as the last: how much they'll miss each other, he'll write as soon as he's settled in, and phone when he can. Their talking stopped when they returned to the car.

After a few gentle kisses and some soft words, their kisses became more passionate. Angie felt his hand slowly easing from her back toward her breasts. When he began to unbutton her blouse, she didn't help but didn't resist. Neither did she resist when he unhooked her bra. His hand seemed so large yet gentle as it caressed her eager breasts. She was trembling with anticipation as he slowly lifted her bra. When he pulled away and admired her bare breasts, she sensed his pleasure. He cuddled one in his hand, leaving her aroused nipple exposed. He kissed her lips, then slowly moved his kisses from her lips to her cheek, her neck, her chest, and finally, to her tender, waiting nipple.

Oh god, I want him. I can't. I have to resist. I have to find the strength.

He removed his hand from her breasts and began moving it down her body.

It's now or never. I have to stop him.

She gently placed her hand on his. "Please." She held it tighter when he continued. "Please stop." He stopped. She left her hand on his as he eased it back to her breasts. She lifted his head and lips from her breasts. "I'm sorry," she whispered. "I just can't."

"I'm sorry," he said, then kissed her gently on the lips. "I guess I was getting a little carried away."

"Me too."

Angie tried to do her homework, but her mind wasn't on homework. She closed the books and, thinking that she would finish in the morning, went to bed. She couldn't sleep. She closed her eyes and was back in Skip's brother's car, in his arms, kissing him passionately. She tingled with desire when she remembered how his lips had slowly moved from hers, then kissed their way to her waiting breasts. Again, she experienced the same surge of pleasure that had rushed through her earlier that night. To break the image of how his lips had felt as they caressed her aroused nipples, she opened her eyes and stared at the ceiling. She was wet with perspiration and her whole body burned with desire. *I have to get control of my feelings and not give in to my desires. I have to.*

～∞～

School was difficult, but work was even more difficult. Angie kept looking at the clock; it seemed slower than usual. Finally, it was nine o'clock. Skip was right on time. They kissed and he asked, "Where would you like to go?"

She wanted to avoid getting into the same situation as the night before. "Do you like boats?"

"I love boats."

"Let's walk out on the docks at the marina and look at the boats."

"Okay."

She sensed, by the sound of his "okay," he was disappointed and had rather drive to the beach and pet. She wanted that too but lacked the confidence to discourage his advances nor was she sure she wanted to. Earlier that day, she had made up her mind to ask to walk on the docks.

They held each other close and walked slowly while admiring the boats. Angie noticed that Skip always stopped at the sailboats and admired them more than the powerboats.

"Have you ever owned a boat?" she asked.

"Yes. My brother and I bought an old, 20' sailboat. It needed a lot of work, so the price was right. We worked on it for at least six months, and when we finished, it looked like new. As we learned more about sailing, we found it to be one of the fastest boats in the area. We were so proud."

"What did you name it?"

"We named her *Fate*. We've spent many days aboard *Fate*. She was our sanctuary when conditions at home became unbearable. Most of the time, we dreaded returning to the dock."

It was obvious to Angie that he enjoyed talking about his boat, but not his life.

"Where is *Fate* now?"

"My brother has her. I was thinking that *Fate* and my brother would be all I'd miss, but not now. I'll miss you even more."

"I'll miss you too."

It was several minutes before either spoke. Skip cleared his throat. It was as if it were tightening, and he was testing his voice before he spoke. "My brother and his wife have returned. They're going to have a little going-away party for me tomorrow night. Can you make it?"

"I wish I could, but Fridays are our busiest night, and it's too late to ask someone to work for me."

"I'd much rather be with you than a silly party, but I don't want to hurt their feelings."

"I understand. Will I see you Saturday?"

"Definitely. Same time?"

"Come early. I might be able to get off a little early."

When they arrived at her car, he asked, "Do you have something to write on?"

"In my car."

"Will you write your address and phone number for me? I don't want to forget to get it." He read her name. "Angela Blake. What a pretty name."

"Isn't it strange that we've had three dates and don't know the other's last name?"

"Yes, it is."

"What's your name?"

"Chastain."

"That's your last name?"

"Yes."

He didn't mention his first, and she didn't ask.

Angie

It was a stormy, overcast night with strong wind and heavy rain. Because of the weather, there were few customers and Angie was able to get off early. Skip arrived at 8:30; Angie was ready to go.

"It looks like April showers have started early," Angie said, as they ran to the car.

"I think you're right."

Skip didn't ask where she wanted to go, and she didn't ask where he was taking her. She knew where.

It was raining too hard to walk on the beach, but Angie didn't mind. This was their last night together, and she had rather be in his arms than walking on the beach.

Neither spoke as they sat silently and listened to the rain falling on the roof and against the windshield. They watched the water flowing down the windshield as if they were in a hypnotic trance. Neither wanted to be first to break the spell.

Angie wondered what he was thinking. She wanted to ask how his going-away party went and much more, but she sensed he was deep in thought. He dropped his hands from the steering wheel and looked toward her. Even in the dim light, she saw a serious expression on his face and in his eyes, almost a look of fear.

He moved to her, gently kissed her, and said, "I love you, Angie."

She was shocked, and before she got control of her thoughts, she wrapped her arms around him and the words left her, "I love you too." She remembered telling herself that she would never express her love until she knew for sure, but it was too late.

They held each other in a tight embrace and kissed. It was a warm, affectionate kiss. A kiss that expressed affection and the disappointment they shared that this was their last night together. She leaned back against the door and cuddled his head to her chest. Except for an occasional kiss on his head, she held him in her arms until the night was black as pitch. She lifted her hand close to her face and thought how this was one of those nights she had heard about—a night so dark you couldn't see your hand in front of your face. The rain intensified, and the sound of it crashing against the roof created a feeling of isolation. And the sound of it driving against the window behind her head added to the passion building inside her.

She felt her T-shirt being pulled from her jeans, then over her breasts. His hand struggled to get to the hook on her bra; to help and without hesitation, she raised her back away from the door. He was cuddling her left breast and kissing its hard, aroused nipple when, as if on cue, a bolt of lightning struck nearby, filling the car with light. The loud clap of thunder caused her to flinch and pull him close to her breasts. As the thunder rolled off in the distance, she sensed his passion building. She was aware of his hand leaving her breasts and slowly moving lower. She put her hand on his but didn't resist, and he didn't stop. He unbuttoned her jeans. When he began pulling her zipper down, she removed her hand. Her body was twitching with desire as he maneuvered his hand beneath her panties.

He lifted his mouth from her breasts and pressed his trembling lips to hers, while at the same time trying to take off her jeans. He lifted off her and she removed her jeans, T-shirt, and underwear. She felt the seat slide back all the way and heard his belt buckle tingle. Even though she was completely nude, she told herself, *It's not too late. I can still stop this. Please don't do this. Please stop while you can.*

As he came to her, she said, "Please, Skip, let's wait." He didn't answer. He was also nude, and it was too late.

℃

Before getting dressed, they held each other until they could no longer stand the cold. Their lovemaking had warmed the car but not enough to be comfortable. The windows had fogged up, and they could no longer see the rain on the windshield or windows, but by the sound on the roof, it had not let up. The lightning and thunder seemed to be off in the distance. The front had passed, and they were left with only rain and plenty of it. Angie moved close to Skip and cuddled up under his arm.

"From now on," she said, "when I see lightning or hear thunder, I'll think of this night."

"So will I. I love you, Angie."

"And I love you."

With his hand caressing her face, he softly kissed her moist lips. She couldn't see his face but felt his warm breath on her lips as he said, "Thanks."

She returned his kiss but didn't answer. She knew what he meant. It was obvious that she was his first. She wished he was hers.

⁓

The rain had almost stopped when they arrived at Angie's car. They sat without talking, looking at the mist on the windshield. Neither wanted the night to end.

"As soon as I get settled in, I'll write and probably every day after." He didn't wait for a response. "I don't know how long it'll be before I can call, but as soon as I can, I will. If I'm only allowed to call at night, can I call you at work?"

"Sure. I might be busy and not able to talk long, but at least I will have heard your voice."

They kissed, opened their doors, and got out. She unlocked the door of her car but didn't open it. She turned to him with tears running down her cheeks and said, "I'm going to miss you so much."

"I'll miss you too."

She went to his open arms. "It'll be the longest eight weeks of my life."

"Mine too."

The rain was increasing. He opened her door and she got in. He leaned in, gently kissed her, and said, "Goodbye, Angie."

"Goodbye, Skip."

CHAPTER 15

Angie had a difficult time concentrating on her work. Each time the phone rang, she was always first to pick it up. *Sooner or later, it will be Skip*. The other employees stopped answering it; it was obvious to them that she was expecting a call. Angie saw Ruby look toward her each time the phone rang, then look away when she answered it; Ruby was concerned. Angie tried to make light of her own concern by telling Ruby that Skip was probably too busy to call.

After three days with no call or letter, Angie had started showing stress, and Ruby began to worry.

When a week had passed, Angie was saying "if" instead of "when" she hears from him, and by the end of the second week, she stopped rushing to the phone.

Ruby tried to encourage her by saying that it had only been two weeks, and she should not give up.

The third week ended with Angie feeling that she was deceived and would never hear from him.

Ruby agreed.

"And," Angie began, "I'm late."

"You're late! You said you weren't going to—"

"I know. But the night before he left, we did. I let passion and desire cloud good judgement."

"You sure as hell did!" Ruby realized, after saying what she did, that instead of criticizing, she should have shown compassion. "I doubt that you're pregnant. You've been under a lot of stress. I'm sure that's the reason."

They didn't speak of Angie's possible condition for the next four weeks but did discuss Skip and what a louse they thought he was. Angie had stopped anticipating the arrival of a letter or phone call and was trying the best she could to get on with her life. To take her mind off Skip, she concentrated on homework and job, but he and the fear of being with child were never far from the surface.

"Well, Ruby. I'm pregnant."

"Are you late again?"

"Way beyond late."

Angie felt the tears forming as Ruby hugged her, and she couldn't keep from crying when Ruby said, "I'm sorry. I'm so sorry, Angie."

"I'm no better than my mother," Angie sobbed.

"Oh, yes, you are. You're nothing like your mother. And don't ever think or say that again. You just had an accident." Angie's crying intensified, and Ruby continued to hold and comfort her. "Let's think positive: we're going to have a baby, and if it looks anything like its mother or father, she or he will be beautiful. Damn, Angie, I'm starting to get excited just thinking about it."

"You're kidding?"

"No, I'm not. There's nothing we can do about it. You aren't planning on doing anything about it, are you?"

"God, no! Of course not."

"Good. Now let's start planning for the blessed event. The first thing you need to do is see a doctor. And not just any doctor. We'll accept nothing but the best. I'll ask around. Now, when the doctor confirms that you're pregnant, and you're convinced you are, let's celebrate and be delighted that this little fellow chose you to be his mother."

"Do you really think that he, or she, chose me to be its mother?"

"No, but it won't hurt to think he did."

"You keep referring to the baby as 'he.'"

"I know. I don't know why, but I think it's going to be a boy."

"I just hope it's healthy."

"It will be, body and mind. We'll make sure of that by always being upbeat and looking forward to his arrival. We don't want to do anything that'll give him the impression he's starting life unwanted. Right?"

"Right."

"You have to promise me that as soon as the doctor tells you you're pregnant, if he does, you will express pleasure in the news. Let your good fortune show. The baby will sense your love and know he's welcome."

"How do you know so much about what babies think?"

"I don't really, but doesn't it sound logical?"

"Yes, it does. I'll do my best."

"Don't worry about a thing. I'll be right here with you. Be proud, think of it as a gift."

"You make it sound so beautiful."

"It will be. Trust me."

Since Angie knew the exact day of conception, the doctor could accurately predict the arrival date. It was December 16.

"I know I promised to be happy," Angie sobbed as Ruby drove her home, "but it's so difficult. All I've worked for...gone. My scholarship. And now my reputation is shot. I wanted my grandmother to be proud of me, and I let her down."

"You haven't let her down. You're keeping the baby, and you know she'd be proud of that. Come on, Angie, stop beating yourself up. If your grandmother were here, she would be as excited as me. And like me, she'd look forward to helping you raise him. There's one thing for sure: between you, Gayle, and me, he will never want for love or attention."

"I still worry about what others will think."

"You've come this far without worrying about what others think. Why should you start now? It's my opinion that the best way to get comfortable is tell everyone you know about your condition. Your classmates, your fellow workers, and anyone else you come in contact with. Let them know you made a mistake, but you love the result. Remember, you don't owe anyone anything. Think of this as the best thing that will ever happen to you, and I truly believe it is."

"Okay, Ruby, I'm ready to start enjoying."

"That's the spirit."

"I think, now that I know for sure, I should try to find Skip and let him know. Don't you?"

"I'd try but not too hard. Where're you going to start?"

"When we get home, I'll look in the phone book."

There were only two listings for Chastain; Angie called both.

"Well?" Ruby asked. "Any luck?"

"They never heard of him."

"That's too bad. You know? That may not even be his real name."

"I've thought of that. If he lied to me about the other things, there's no reason to think he wouldn't lie about his name. I'm going to put him out of my mind and concentrate on raising our baby."

"I wouldn't even include him as being part of the baby."

"I wasn't. I meant yours and mine."

"I love you, Angie."

"I love you too."

Like Ruby suggested, Angie told everyone important to her about being pregnant and how pleased she was. They may have expressed different thoughts behind her back, but when they talked with her, everyone seemed pleased and understanding.

Not long after Angie's graduation ceremonies, she began to show. She continued to work even though she was getting larger. One day, the owner of the restaurant asked to see her in his office. She was worried.

"Hi, Angie," he said as he arranged her chair, "how are you feeling?"

"Hi, Mr. Martin. I'm fine. And thanks for asking."

"Please. Call me Gary."

"Okay, Gary."

"I want you to know that I really admire how you're dealing with your situation. You are extremely courageous."

"I have to give a lot of credit to Ruby. Without her, it would not have been this easy."

"Ruby is one helluva young lady. She certainly won't take any crap from anyone, will she?"

"No, she won't." Angie was becoming even more nervous. She knew he didn't ask her to come to his office to make small talk.

"Angie, I have a big favor to ask. I won't be offended if you say no. But I'll be extremely pleased if you say yes." He paused for a moment. "My wife is very sick. She has leukemia."

"Oh my god! I'm so sorry."

"We don't know how much longer she has: maybe six months, maybe a year, we just don't know. As you know, my hours are long, and occasionally I have to go out of town. I need someone to be with her full time. I would like that someone to be you."

"Oh, I don't know. I'm not sure I'm the one you're looking for."

"Please don't say no. At least give it a try. You'll have your own area that's separate from the main living area. You can go and come as you like, as long as you're not gone too long. You can have Ruby and your other girlfriends over. In fact, my wife would love for you to have Ruby over. The two of you would cheer her up, and she needs that. I'm not looking for a maid or a nurse, I'm looking for someone to be my wife's friend, and with your personality and compassion, you'd be perfect. And your pay would increase considerably."

"I don't know. Ruby and I have such big plans for my baby. I'd hate to disappoint her."

"You can still make your plans and use our house as if it were your own. But if it doesn't work out to your satisfaction, you can leave anytime you like. You'll still have your job here no matter what you decide."

"I'd like to discuss this with Ruby. Can I let you know tomorrow?"

"Sure. Before you say no, will you come with me and meet my wife?"

"When?"

"It's early. We can go now or we can go tomorrow, after you talk with Ruby."

She thought for a moment. "Now will be good."

"I was hoping you'd say that."

⁓

Gary talked continuously about his wife, and by the time they arrived at his home, Angie knew everything of any importance, and some that wasn't, about his wife. She knew her age, how they met, how long they had been married, and they couldn't have children—he was the reason, not her. He told her about his wife's illness and how she didn't want to prolong it with treatments that would make her sick without any guarantee of extending her life. His voice expressed the love and admiration he had for his wife and grief when he spoke of her condition. Angie felt sorry for him and his wife as he described their perfect marriage—one ending long before it should. Even before they arrived, she felt certain she was going to stay.

While Gary was talking, Angie had been thinking how Rev. Buchanan helped her and her grandmother in their time of need and how much she appreciated his support. Now, this was her chance to help someone in need, and she looked forward to the opportunity.

⁓

Gary's wife was lying on the sofa watching television; the back blocked her view of them.

"You're home early," she said without getting up.

"I have someone I'd like you to meet."

"Angie?" she asked as she stood and faced them.

"Yes. Angie."

"Hi, Angie. I'm Susan. I've been looking forward to meeting you." Instead of shaking Angie's extended hand, she chose to ignore it and embraced her. "Gary has told me so much about you. Come sit with me on the sofa."

"Can I get you ladies something to drink?" Gary asked as he walked toward the kitchen.

"No, thank you," Angie answered.

"I'll have a glass of tea," Susan said, then turned to Angie. "I understand you're expecting."

"Yes. If everything goes well, he or she will arrive around the middle of December."

"I'm so proud of you. Gary told me about your situation and how you're dealing with it."

"My girlfriend, Ruby, has encouraged me to think of my condition as a gift."

"I agree with Ruby. Gary often speaks of Ruby. I can't wait to meet her. You will have her over, won't you?" Before Angie could answer, Susan said, "Let me show you where you'll be staying if you choose to be our guest. And a guest is how I prefer you think of your stay. I'm not sure if you've made up your mind, but ever since Gary told me how impressed he is with you, I've been hoping you will."

As they walked and even before they arrived at the area of the house Susan was taking her, Angie said, "I'll stay."

Susan abruptly stopped, threw her arms around her, and while they hugged, said, "Thank you, Angie. Thank you so much. You've made me so happy."

"I feel very comfortable with you and your husband, and I'm looking forward to living with you. I had planned to talk with Ruby, but I don't need to. Now, let's check out my room."

"Gary!" Susan shouted. "Angie is staying with us."

"Hot damn!" Gary shouted from the kitchen. "Thanks, Angie."

Angie's room was separated from the rest of the house and extremely large. It had a queen-sized bed, a lounge chair, another comfortable chair, and a desk. A spacious private bathroom joined the room and there was plenty of closet space. It reminded Angie of the plush hotel rooms she had seen in magazines and on television.

Susan showed Angie where the towels and linens were, then asked, "What do you think?"

Angie smiled. "I think I can make this do."

Gary and Susan's smile expressed their pleasure.

"Welcome home," they both said at the same time.

"Where have you been?" Ruby asked when Angie arrived home. "I was beginning to worry."

"I'm sorry. I should've let you know where I was going when I left the restaurant, but I thought I'd be back before you left. I went with Gary, our boss, to meet his wife."

"To meet his wife?"

"Yes. She's very sick and they want me to move in with them and help take care of her. Actually, they want me to be more like a companion, someone to share her day with."

"How long do they think she'll be sick?"

"She'll never get well. She only has six months to a year to live."

"Bummer. You're going to move in, aren't you?"

"I just have to, Ruby. I couldn't say no. Susan, that's her name, is such a wonderful person. She's anxious to meet you. From what she tells me, her husband talks about us all the time."

"What if you're not as pleased as you think you'll be? And what about your baby?"

"I can leave anytime I like. And I plan to come home about two weeks before its time and be with you."

"That sounds perfect."

"You aren't upset, are you?"

"Oh no. I was planning to talk with you tonight about something, and the timing is perfect. As you know, Carl and I are planning to get married, and we were wondering if after we're married, you would mind if we live here with you? We will pay whatever the rent would be if we rented an apartment."

"Of course you can. You know you don't have to ask."

"We didn't want to take it for granted."

"Me leaving will work out perfectly," Angie said. "That'll give you newlyweds some privacy. Now, when is the date? I have a wedding to put together."

"Oh no, you don't! We are going to have a very small ceremony, with no one attending but you, Gayle, and one of Carl's friends. One of my regular customers is a notary public, and tonight, Carl and I asked him to marry us. He agreed. We set the date for two weeks from today. We were hoping to have the wedding here in your home."

"Can Gayle and I decorate just a little?"

"A little."

"You're right. Things are working out perfectly."

"When are you moving in with Susan?"

"I'll move some of my things tomorrow. I don't want to move too much. I may not want to stay."

"I'll help you. I don't have to work tomorrow."

"That'll be great. Then you can meet Susan."

CHAPTER 16

While Angie was getting organized and putting her clothes and other belongings away, Ruby talked with Susan. By their laughter and the parts of their conversation Angie could hear, it was obvious that Susan and Ruby were enjoying each other's company.

"All finished?" Susan asked when Angie joined them.

"For now. I'll get the rest of my stuff as I need it."

"How about we take a swim in the pool? You did bring your bathing suits, didn't you?"

"I didn't," Ruby answered.

"You can use one of mine," Angie suggested.

"I couldn't possibly get into one of yours. And besides, if I did, I would stretch it out of shape, and I wouldn't want to do that."

"You might as well stretch one. It won't be long before I'll be stretching them."

"I don't think one of your suits would cover enough of my body. But I would like to go swimming, so let's go home and get one of mine."

On the way home, Ruby said, "I can see why you accepted their offer. And like you said, Susan is a wonderful person. I was a little leery about their intentions. I thought they might be taking advantage of you. I'm glad to say I was wrong."

Angie, Ruby, and Susan had a fun-filled day. They swam in the pool and had a light lunch, but mostly they talked about Angie's upcoming arrival and Ruby's wedding. It was late in the afternoon when Ruby said she had to be leaving.

Ruby hugged Susan and said, "I know I said I want a small wedding, but you are invited and I really want you to come."

"If Angie can get me there, I'll be there."

Angie's look expressed her appreciation that Ruby had asked. "She'll be there."

It only took Angie a few days to feel comfortable in her new environment. Susan took a nap in the morning and one in the afternoon; that's when Angie cleaned the house and checked and cleaned the pool. Angie also washed and polished her Mustang during Susan's naps. She kept it looking good for when Susan would say, "Let's go cruise the beach."

At least once a week, Susan asked to go cruising; she preferred to ride with the top down. Not only did they go cruising in Angie's car, they used it to go shopping and to the many appointments Susan had with her doctor. While backing out of the driveway, Susan always said, "I love this car. It makes me feel young."

Occasionally, Gary brought home something to eat from the restaurant, but mostly, Angie did the cooking. She loved to cook and Susan enjoyed her cooking. Sometimes, Susan joined Angie in the kitchen and they experimented with some of her exotic recipes, but mostly their meals were fairly basic. Shrimp was Susan's favorite, so they had shrimp at least once a week, usually grilled.

Susan and Angie became extremely close. They did everything together. Angie enjoyed Susan's company as much as Susan enjoyed being with her. Angie thought of Susan as a close companion and friend and never thought of her as an employer. They were very much aware of the other's love and respect. They were as close as sisters.

Soon after Ruby's wedding, Susan began feeling the effects of her illness. Each day was worse than the day before. Angie held her arm and supported her when they went shopping, helped her out of her chair and bed, and there were fewer joy rides in the Mustang. The joy rides eventually stopped, and Angie went shopping alone. Susan stayed in bed most of the day.

The last two weeks before Angie's baby was to arrive, Susan was very sick and in a lot of pain but refused to be admitted to the hospital; she wanted to be home when the baby arrived. Gary didn't want Angie to do any lifting, so he was home more often than not. He helped Susan when she had to use the bathroom and when she bathed.

Angie couldn't believe how tired and expressionless Susan looked. While sitting on the side of Susan's bed and trying to give the impression of being upbeat and not noticing how close to death she looked, Angie said, "I wonder how close the doctor's prediction will be?"

"What's the date?"

"The fourteenth."

Susan slowly turned her face toward the ceiling and whispered, "Two more days." Her eyes looked as if they were looking through the ceiling. "I hope I make it."

"You'll make it, with months to spare."

"I doubt that. But that was kind of you to say." She paused then asked, "Have you chosen a name?"

"If it's a girl and if it's okay with you, I'm going to name her Susan. I'll call her Sue. If it's a boy, I haven't decided."

"Thank you, Angie. I'm so glad you chose to live with us. I have a favor to ask. If it's a boy, will you name him Kenneth? That was my father's name."

"I feel certain it's a boy. And Kenneth is his name."

"Thanks, Angie."

Angie knocked on Gary and Susan's bedroom door: it was three o'clock in the morning and the sixteenth. Gary opened the door, and while tying the belt on his robe, he asked, "Is it time?"

"I think so."

"I'll get dressed."

"You better stay here with Susan. I'll call Ruby. We've been planning for this day."

"Are you sure?"

"Yes. Susan needs you more than I."

Kenneth was born that afternoon, December 16. Ruby was waiting in Angie's room when they wheeled her in.

"Hi, Mom. How you feeling?"

"A lot better, now that it's over. Have you seen him?"

"Only through the nursery glass. He's a handsome baby."

"He's not handsome. He's beautiful."

"No. He's handsome."

"He looks a lot like his father," Angie said. "Don't you agree?"

"Yes, I do, but I didn't want to be the first to say it."

"I know one thing—from the difficult time I had and the way I feel now—he definitely has his father's shoulders."

Ruby laughed, then hugged her. "You're something else, and I love you."

"Here's the big man," the nurse said as she entered the room. "It's time for dinner."

"Hi, Kenny," Ruby said. "Can I hold him?"

The nurse paused and looked at Angie.

"Mothers are normally first."

"I held him in the delivery room."

The nurse gently placed him in Ruby's waiting arms, smiled, and said, "Try to not let your tears drown him."

Ruby returned the nurse's smile, then wiped her tears with her shoulders. "I'll be careful." She held him for several minutes without talking, just admiring. "You're so pretty. Yes, you are. Do you want to go to your mommy and get some din-din?"

The nurse took him and placed him in Angie's arms, then helped her give him the first taste of his mother's milk.

Angie and Ruby were smiling and admiring Kenneth as he nursed when suddenly, Angie's expression changed. She looked up at Ruby. "How's Susan?"

"She's holding on."

"I want her to see Kenny."

"She will. I just imagine that's what she's waiting for."

⌇

Ruby was carrying Kenny while Gary helped Angie in the house. When they were safely in, Angie took her baby and went into Susan's room. Susan lifted her arms and smiled as Angie approached. Angie laid him next to Susan. "Kenny, I want you to meet your Aunt Susan."

Susan cradled him between her arm and chest. "Oh, Angie. He's beautiful." She touched his chin, then his nose. "Don't worry, Kenny. Someday, when you're older, people will call you Ken. But for now, you're our little Kenny." She talked to him a few minutes more, then closed her eyes. She didn't move when Angie lifted Kenny from her embrace. Gary gently shook her, but she didn't wake. He looked at Ruby and said, "Call the ambulance. The number is by the phone."

When Ruby returned, Gary was sitting on the side of the bed, holding his wife's hand, and Angie was standing beside him, holding Kenny. Ruby reached for Kenny, but Angie didn't want to let him go. Ruby put her arm around her. "You need to lie down. Come on, I'll help you to your room."

"I should be with her," Angie said as she laid Kenny in his bassinet.

"There's nothing you can do. And you certainly don't want your last memory of her to be seeing her carried out on a stretcher."

"You're right."

⌇

Susan had left explicit instructions with Gary and Angie about what to do after her death. She wanted no more than a brief mention of her death in the obituary section, no service whatsoever, and wished to go straight to the crematorium. She had said, "If my friends don't have a funeral to attend or flowers to send, it'll be as if I never left." She never mentioned any instructions to Angie about what to do with her ashes. Angie assumed Gary was told, but she didn't ask.

Two days after Susan's death, Angie and Gary were talking. Angie said, "I guess it's time I move back home."

"I wish you wouldn't. Not yet."

"But—"

"I realize you think that since Susan is no longer here, there's no need for you to be here, but there is. The house and I need you, it would seem empty without you, and I'd really miss you and Kenny. Just for a few more weeks. Please?"

"I would love to stay, but are you sure?"

"Yes, I'm sure. Besides, if you leave, Susan's plants and flowers will die from lack of love and water, and we don't want that. Do we?"

"You'd water them."

"Maybe and maybe not. But one thing for sure, they wouldn't get the same love and attention that you and Susan gave them. They'd miss you."

Angie laughed. "I'll stay, but only to save the plants."

He smiled and patted the back of her hand. "Thanks, Angie." He paused for a moment. "You and Kenny will be here a lot more than me, so think of the house as your home. You know how hectic my work is and how unpredictable my hours are, and now that I don't have Susan to come home to, I'll probably be away even more. Your friends, Ruby and Gayle, are welcome here as often as you or they desire."

"More than likely," Angie said, "Gayle will be here often. Her being here will help keep me from missing Susan."

"If she'd like to stay over, there's always the third bedroom."

"Thanks. But I doubt that she'll be staying over."

Angie

It was a bittersweet Christmas for all. They grieved Susan's death and, at the same time, celebrated the birth of Kenny. Ruby and Gayle had decorated Angie's house, which was now called Ruby and Carl's home, and prepared a large Christmas dinner. Even though Gary's house was larger, Ruby felt the atmosphere at her home was more festive and with fewer recent memories.

After the presents were opened and they had finished the excellent dinner Ruby and Gayle had prepared, Gary cheered up and became less despondent. It wasn't long before he joined in the conversations and the laughter. It pleased Angie to see that he was enjoying the evening. She felt it was the closure he needed.

It was a quiet ride home. Gary drove without talking while Angie held Kenny and reminisced about the evening. She felt the warmth from her baby against her chest as he lay sleeping in her arms. Knowing her friends had helped Gary through a trying time brought her comfort, and she knew he appreciated their efforts. She thought how lucky she was to have friends like Ruby, Gayle, and Carl, how close she and Gary had become, and how much comfort and support they brought to each other since her son's birth and Susan's death.

She took her eyes off her baby and looked at the rain falling against the windshield, the wipers moving barely fast enough to keep up. She watched as the water built up and how before her vision of the street ahead was blurred, the wipers wiped it away. She looked down at her son, and for the first time in a long time, she felt secure and content.

"Thanks, Angie."

The sound of Gary's voice startled her. She looked at him and smiled. She didn't answer. She understood.

CHAPTER 17

Most mornings, Ruby helped Angie with Kenny, and in the afternoons, after school, Gayle helped. It wasn't that Angie needed their help, even though it was appreciated, they just enjoyed being with Kenny. Because he was awake most of the day, from all their attention, it wasn't long before he was sleeping all night, which Angie welcomed.

Angie saw very little of Gary; he stayed busy at his restaurant. After a few months of almost constant work, he was showing signs of exhaustion. Angie was beginning to worry.

One night while having one of their few dinners together, Angie asked, "Don't you think you're working a little too hard?"

"Probably. But how else can I keep my mind off Susan?"

"I don't know, but I do know if you continue to manage your restaurant alone, you're going to get yourself into a situation you can't get out of."

"What do you suggest?"

"You probably think I'm a know-it-all, smart-ass, and should stay out of your business."

"No. No. I value your opinion. Please, what do you suggest?"

She thought for a moment. "You have some good, loyal employees, and I feel certain they can manage without you. Don't you?"

"Yes, I'm sure they could."

"Then, how 'bout you come home for dinner at least two nights a week. And one day a week, you don't go in at all. You pick the days, but make sure they are the same days each week. That way, everyone at the restaurant and I can adapt. On the nights you're off, I'll prepare

"I didn't know you were a boater."

"I've always loved boats, especially sailboats. I've owned a few, but that was several years ago. There's nothing more relaxing than the silence of sailing when all you hear is the boat cutting through the water and the waves slapping against the hull. You'll see."

The engine slowed, and they joined the owner in the cockpit.

"Take the tiller, Gary, and hold her in the wind," the owner said. "I'll hoist the sails."

"Can I help?" Angie asked.

"I got her, but thanks for asking," the owner said as he went forward.

When the mainsail was up and secured, Gary took a few turns around the winch with the mainsheet and hauled it in. He did the same when the jib was hoisted and secured.

"Looks like you've sailed before," the owner said when he joined them in the cockpit.

"Yes, but it's been a few years."

When the owner turned off the engine, Angie couldn't believe the silence. She felt her smile get larger and her excitement build as the boat began to heel and its speed increased. She saw that Gary's eyes and smile were expressing his pleasure when he asked, "What do you think?"

"I love it!" After answering him, she thought how they should contain their excitement. *If the owner knows how much we like the boat, he may be reluctant to negotiate the price.*

Something ahead caught the owner's eye. "See that boat ahead?" Angie and Gary looked forward. "Watch how fast we overtake and pass him."

Gary trimmed the jib for the new direction; the owner trimmed the main. Angie couldn't believe how fast they passed the other boat. She heard Gary say, "Not bad," but she didn't look at him; she didn't want the owner to see that she was impressed.

"Prepare to come about!" the owner commanded. Angie watched as Gary untied the jib sheet. The owner shouted, "Hard a lee." When the time was right, Gary loosened the sheet, then went to the other side and hauled in the other. The owner chose a direction, and Gary fine-tuned the jib while the owner adjusted the main. Angie saw that Gary was pleased with how the boat handled. She knew he had to have her.

After several more maneuvers, they headed back to the marina. Gary sailed her back. On the way, he asked the owner several questions, and they negotiated the price. By the time they reached the marina, they had agreed on a price. Gary and the owner shook hands and set a time to meet at the bank the next day to finalize the deal.

Angie and Gary were barely in the car when she shouted, "God, that was fun! And I can't believe that," she snapped her fingers, "just that quick, you own a boat! What are you going to name her?"

"I don't know."

"She sure was a remedy for the depressed state you were in."

"You're right. She did bring me pleasure."

"Why don't you name her *Remedy*?"

"I like that. *Remedy* she is."

Angie noticed that he wasn't driving in the direction of home. "Where are we going?"

"I want to show you something."

It wasn't long before she sensed he was taking her to Longboat Key.

"Something on Longboat?"

"Yes."

They were only a few miles from Longboat Pass when he turned off the main road. Angie's curiosity was getting to her. "Do you know someone in this area?"

"No, I don't."

They were almost to the end of the road when he pulled off and into the trees. He turned off the engine.

"What do you think?"

"About what?"

"About this piece of property."

"It's gorgeous, but why are you asking?"

"It's mine. I own it."

"You own this?"

"Yes. I've owned it for several years."

Angie was first out of the car and walked straight to the canal at the back of the property. She was standing on the seawall looking out over Sarasota Bay when Gary joined her.

"Is this where you're going to keep *Remedy?*"

"Yes. As soon as I get a dock built."

"What a view," she said as they looked out over the bay. They turned and looked back at the property. "When are you planning to build?"

"I hadn't planned to build anytime soon, but I think I'll start designing a home today."

"That's a super idea. Designing and building a house will definitely occupy your mind. Do you have a design in mind?"

"Somewhat. What do you say we get something to eat, then drive around and look at houses until you have to be home to feed Kenny?"

"I love looking at houses."

"Good. I can see that you're going to be a big help."

Gary found a dock builder who wasn't busy. He told Gary the dock would be finished by the weekend. On Tuesday, Angie had dinner ready early so they could go see *Remedy* while there was still plenty of light. Thursday, she did the same, and they went to the property to see the dock. While inspecting the dock, which was almost finished, Gary said, "The dock will be completed by this weekend, so what do you say you, Kenny, and I move *Remedy* this Sunday?"

"Do you think the two of us can handle her *and* Kenny?"

"Of course we can. Here, let me hold Kenny, your arm has to be getting tired."

As she handed Kenny to Gary, she said, "Wouldn't you be more comfortable with someone who knew more about sailing than me?"

"No, I wouldn't. We can make a bed for this little fellow on the floor of the cabin. That way, he won't fall off the berth when we heel over. And when you have to be with him, I can handle *Remedy*."

"We could ask Ruby and Carl to join us."

"I'd really prefer our maiden voyage to be just us. We can handle her. Trust me."

"I trust you."

Angie had Kenny's clean clothes and diapers packed, the sandwiches were prepared, and drinks were in the cooler, all by the time Gary showered. While she made breakfast, Gary loaded his car. They had planned for Angie to leave her car at the property, then drive Gary's to the marina. They would pick his car up later that evening.

The first thing they did when they arrived at the marina was fix a safe place for Kenny. Once Kenny was comfortable and playing with his toys, Angie and Gary unloaded his car and organized the boat. Even before Gary started the engine, he patiently explained some of the rigging and its purpose. He taught her how to tie a line to a cleat and much more. He started the engine, and while it was warming, they untied the lines from the dock. When the engine had warmed, they shoved off.

After they had motored out of the marina, Gary encouraged Angie to take the tiller, and while she was getting comfortable with steering, he stowed the lines in the lazaret. He showed her the wind indicator at the top of the mast, then instructed her on how to hold *Remedy* into the wind while he hoisted the sails. When the sails were up, he turned off the engine.

"That wasn't so hard, was it?" he asked.

"Did I do good?"

"You did good."

He trimmed the sails and taught her how to keep the sails full by watching the tell-tails.

"Do you want to take the tiller?" Angie asked.

"Only if you want me to."

"Not really. I love to steer."

"Then you are our helmsman or helmswoman."

Not only did Angie watch the tell-tails, the sails, and where she was going, she watched Kenny. Each time she tacked and the boat heeled to the opposite side, she looked in the cabin to make sure he had adjusted to the change. On one of her tacks, she noticed that Kenny was beginning to fuss; he was four months old and still nursing.

"I'm going below," she said. "It's time for Kenny and me to share our special time."

Gary took the tiller. "I'll take her. Kenny has really been good, hasn't he?"

She picked him up. "Yes, he has. He's my little sailor."

Angie closed the companionway door for privacy, and while she was feeding Kenny, Gary headed *Remedy* for her new home.

By the time they were tied to the dock and picked up Gary's car, it was getting late.

Angie fed Kenny while Gary fixed them a light dinner. All through dinner and even after, Angie couldn't stop asking questions about sailing and sailboats.

"I can't believe how patient you were with me."

"When I was a young boy, I used to crew on a race boat. The owner never explained what he expected of his crew, he just screamed at us when we did something he didn't approve of. As you can imagine, he couldn't keep a crew and never won a race. I promised myself that I would always be patient and never raise my voice to someone unfamiliar with sailing. If I raise my voice, it's because we're in trouble and I need your attention."

"You'd make an excellent father."

"Maybe. But that's all behind me. It just wasn't in the cards."

"I'm sorry. How old are you…if you don't mind me asking?"

"I don't mind. I'm thirty-three. And, if I remember right, you're eighteen."

"In two months, I'll be nineteen on the tenth of June."

"Well, how about that! June 7, I'll be thirty-four. We can celebrate our birthdays together."

Angie asked several more questions, then said, "It's been a long but memorable day, and I'm getting sleepy. I'm going to turn in."

"I won't be far behind."

CHAPTER 18

While having breakfast and without warning or reason, Angie said, "Don't you think I should be going home and let you get on with your life? You have plenty to do without me and my baby holding you back. You have a boat to enjoy and a house to build, and I feel that Kenny and I will just be in your way."

"The last thing you need to worry about is being in my way. Look, I'm eating a delicious breakfast that I wouldn't be having if you weren't here, my house is clean, and I look forward to the delicious meals and the relaxing evenings you create on Tuesdays and Thursdays. I love Kenny as if he were my own son, and I would miss him almost as much as I'd miss you. So if you don't have a really good reason to leave…"

"I just don't want to become a problem for you."

"Please, Angie, don't ever think that you are or have been a problem. You were the best friend and companion Susan could've hoped for, and I will be forever grateful. Now I feel that you and Kenny are the best thing that could happen to me. I wish you hadn't stopped me from compensating you after Susan passed away. Will you reconsider?"

"Oh no. I could never accept money for staying with you. I'd never want you to think I'm staying here for the money. Besides, the money you spend on Kenny and me now is probably more than my salary was. Kenny and I have a comfortable house to live in, we have our food and other necessities furnished, and you even pay for the maintenance and gas for my car. And because of that, I'm able to put all the rent money I receive from Ruby and Carl in my savings account. A girl couldn't have it much better than that."

"You're staying?"

"I'm staying."

"Good. So that you'll be comfortable staying with me, I'll make you a promise: if I become uncomfortable with you and Kenny, I will let you know. And I'd like you to promise me that if you become uncomfortable with me or staying here, you will let me know. That way, we can go our separate ways before our friendship is affected."

"I promise."

Gary finished his breakfast, and as he was headed for the door, he asked, "What are your plans for today?"

"Ruby will be coming over before she goes to work. We've been talking about going to see our friend, Wayne. He hasn't seen Kenny yet. I think today will be a good day to go for a visit."

"Have fun. I'll see you tonight."

While Angie was pregnant and after Kenny's birth, she had kept in touch with Wayne by phone, but for one reason or another, they had not visited. Early into her pregnancy, she had informed him of her condition, but it was never mentioned again.

Even though Angie had called, she and Ruby were surprised to see Wayne standing in his driveway waiting for them. He waved as Ruby pulled into his drive, then positioned himself to be at Angie's door when they stopped. He opened the door, leaned in and kissed her, said hello to Ruby, then gently lifted Kenny from Angie's arms.

"Hi, Kenny. Wow! You're a big boy."

Ruby joined them. "How have you been?" she asked as she kissed Wayne on the cheek.

"I've missed seeing you girls, but other than that, I'm doing fine." After admiring Kenny and talking to him, he said, "Come in. Come in. Let's get out of this hot sun."

Angie

Angie had always admired Wayne's house, and now that Gary was trying to come up with a good house plan, she evaluated it with even more interest. "Did you design your house?"

"No. A good friend of mine did. Why do you ask?"

"Gary, the friend I'm staying with, is going to be building a house, and he's looking for some good ideas."

"He needs to talk to my friend, Bill. He is the best architect in the area."

"What's his name?"

"Bill Whitmer. I don't have his number, but he's listed in the Sarasota section of the phone book. It'll be listed as William Whitmer. Before Gary wastes any more time trying to come up with a plan, I suggest he call Bill. He will be surprised at how much help Bill can be."

"Who built your house?"

"Bill Bentz. I highly recommend him. He's listed in the Bradenton section."

"I'll give Gary those names."

"He won't be disappointed."

That night when Gary arrived, Angie mentioned how much she had enjoyed her visit with Wayne and how impressed she was with his home. She described his home, then mentioned how Wayne had suggested that Gary give his architect and builder a call. His smile expressed his appreciation.

"I'll call them tomorrow."

The next day, as usual, but earlier, Gary called home. Angie sensed a more than normal upbeat tone to his voice when he inquired about how she and Kenny were and how their day was going. He gave her time to answer, then asked, "Are you doing something that you can't stop?"

"No."

"I called Bill Whitmer, the architect, and he can meet with us this afternoon."

"Us?"

"Yes, us. I'll pick you and Kenny up in about fifteen minutes. Will that give you enough time?"

"I'll be ready."

"See you in fifteen."

She was thrilled that Gary wanted her to be with him and a part of his new home. She rushed to Kenny's room and hurriedly packed what she thought he might need.

⌒

Gary introduced Angie to Bill as a close friend and someone whose opinion he valued. Kenny was sleeping in Angie's arms. Gary spread Kenny's blanket on the sofa in Bill's office and Angie laid her sleeping son on it. As she shook Bill's hand, she wondered what he really thought of her and Gary's relationship. She returned to the sofa and sat close to Kenny. Gary sat in a chair; Bill sat at his drawing board.

Angie patiently listened to Gary and Bill as they discussed lot size, floor plans, rooflines, and various house styles. To get an idea of the type of house Gary desired, Bill asked him many questions, and more often than not, Gary would ask Angie for her opinion. Before answering, she gave each question a lot of thought and always had an intelligent answer. She never said something like "I don't care," "Whatever you want," or "It's your house." It wasn't long before Bill realized that Angie's input was of value to both him and Gary and began directing his questions to her as well as Gary.

Bill turned toward his drawing board and began sketching.

"How about looking at this and tell me what you think?" Gary stood to join him. "You too, Angie."

With Angie on one side and Gary on the other, Bill described his sketches. "This is just an idea to see if this is the type of house you have in mind."

Gary checked out the drawings. "Yes. That's exactly what we're looking for. Right, Angie?"

"It's what you've been talking about." She tried to answer without sounding as if she expected to be included in his new home.

"Before I get started, if you hire me, the first thing I need to do is look at the property."

Angie went back to the sofa while they discussed Bill's fee. She was impressed with Bill and was pleased when she heard Gary say, "You're hired." Bill said he was just finishing a job and could start in a few days.

When Gary called, Angie heard the excitement in his voice. It had been three days since their visit with Bill.

"Bill has some sketches ready for us to look at."

"Great!"

"Can you pick them up this afternoon? That way, I can check them out when I get home tonight."

"Sure. Kenny just woke up, so I'll leave now."

Bill went over the drawings with Angie; she was impressed. She couldn't believe how much he had accomplished in such a short time. He told her how much he liked Gary's property and how he had come up with a floor plan that took advantage of the spectacular view. She asked many questions and made notes, all while holding Kenny.

When they finished going over the floor plan, the elevations, and the location of the pool, Bill said, "It's rare to work with someone that can grasp the feel of a design as quickly as you. Gary is fortunate to have you helping him."

"Thanks, but it's not my ability. Your drawings are easy to understand."

"I work with many people and I seldom find someone as quick as you. Trust me. You are above average." He rolled up a set of prints, then said, "You and Gary look these over and get back to me with any changes you'd like to make. As soon as we finalize our ideas with this smaller scale, I'll start the larger scale for the finished drawings."

That night, Angie and Gary went over the drawings. They made only a few changes. The next morning, Angie returned the prints. Bill agreed with the changes and said he would get started on the final drawings.

For the next few weeks, Angie stayed busy researching cabinet shops, tile and marble stores, window and door suppliers, and much more. In the evenings and after dinner, she and Gary would sit at the dining room table and check out the brochures and information she had accumulated during the day. When a decision was made, Angie would return the next day to Bill's office and inform him. He would add their suggestions to the specifications and, more often than not, present her with another challenge. Then off she'd go, looking for bathroom fixtures or something else.

Angie always made sure Kenny had eaten and was dry before going to visit Bill. She didn't want him to be fussing and disturb them while she informed Bill of Gary's ideas and changes.

Bill's office was in his home, and from his driveway, Angie could see him sitting at his drawing board and he could see her. Soon after pulling into his drive, Bill or his wife, Roslyn, or both were there to help her with Kenny, his diaper bag, and the many magazines and drawings. Bill had told her that he looked forward to her visits; her cheerful enthusiasm was a welcome change from most of his clients.

Roslyn always welcomed the opportunity to hold and entertain Kenny while Angie talked with her husband. She had told Angie that she couldn't believe how, at only nineteen, she was the responsible mother she was. Each time she took Kenny from Angie, she kissed his head and said, "God, you smell good."

Angie

〜

It took Bill close to four weeks to finish the drawings, and during that time, Angie visited him two or three times a week. When Gary and Angie went to pick up the finished plans, Bill mentioned how it had been a pleasure working for them and how lucky Gary was to have someone helping him as energetic and responsible as Angie. He also told Angie how impressed he was with her ability to visualize the finished product and suggested that she pursue a career in interior design or some other form of design.

"Thanks for your kind remarks," Angie said as they hugged. "I'll miss my visits with you and Roslyn."

Roslyn joined them, shook Gary's hand, then she and Angie hugged.

"I'll miss you and Kenny," she said. "Come see us."

"We will."

As Bill rolled up the drawings and put them in a tube, he asked, "Have you talked with a contractor about building your home?"

"Yes. I plan to meet with Bill Bentz next week and finalize the contract."

"Good. You can't do better than Bill. He's the best."

〜

It was several weeks before Bentz Construction began building Gary's home. While waiting for the construction to begin, Angie spent most of her time cleaning and preparing *Remedy* for their customary Sunday cruise. When construction did start, Angie only went to see the progress with Gary, and that was on Tuesday and Thursday evenings. On Sunday, before and after they went sailing, she and Gary spent additional time looking at the results of that week's work. Not until the workers began finishing the inside did Angie start getting involved.

CHAPTER 19

It was the middle of November and three months earlier, when Kenny was eight months old, Angie stopped breastfeeding and began feeding him from a bottle. She no longer had to find a secluded place to feed him, and her breasts were dry and back to normal. She welcomed the extra time but missed the quiet bonding experience of being close and alone with her baby. She especially missed feeding him when they went sailing.

Her most cherished memories were aboard *Remedy*, in the cabin with the companionway door closed, admiring the contented look on her baby's face as he enjoyed his mother's milk and watching his eyelids slowly close then quickly open as he fought to stay awake. But no matter how hard he fought, the relaxing sound of the hull rushing through the water encouraged his eyes to stay closed while the waves gently rocked him to sleep.

Angie looked forward to Tuesdays and Thursdays; Gary was still coming home early on those days. She always had something prepared for dinner that would keep until they returned from inspecting Gary's house. After dinner, when Gary was helping Angie clear the table and putting the dishes in the dishwasher, they occasionally brushed against each other. Angie found that each accidental touch was enjoyed more than the last. And it was obvious that Gary was savoring the occasional contact as much as she. It wasn't long before their touching and brushing became more deliberate than accidental. They both realized something was happening, but neither wanted to be first to mention what they felt.

Angie frequently reminded herself of the fifteen-year difference in their age, and it had not even been a year since Susan passed away. Most nights, she lay awake struggling to identify her feelings. She wondered if she was misreading her comfort and his respect as something more.

She felt certain that because of their difference in age and so soon after Susan's death, he thought of her as someone he was comfortable being with and would not allow himself to think of her as anything but a close friend. She made herself a promise that she would not say or do anything to cause him to think she desired more than being his friend.

⌒⌿⌒

Angie and Gary had returned from a wonderful day of sailing. *Remedy* was tied to the dock, and Kenny was still aboard, sleeping on his pallet in the cabin. Angie and Gary were standing on the dock, looking toward his new home. The pool was started, and the house was close to being finished. They stood without talking as they admired what had been accomplished. The late afternoon air was a little cool, and when a cool misty breeze rolled in off the bay, Angie felt chilled and wrapped her arms together across her chest. Gary moved closer and put his arm around her. She wanted to unwrap her arms and put them around him, but chose to leave them folded on her chest.

They stood like that for several minutes without talking, just looking toward the house. Angie sensed, by the affectionate tightening of his arm as he caressed her close to his side, that he was not only trying to warm her, he was going to say something.

"I love you, Angie."

She unfolded her arms, wrapped them around his waist, and pressed her cheek against his chest. "I love you too."

They silently held each other for several minutes. She lifted her face from his chest and looked into his yearning eyes. Their lips parted and came together. It was not a passionate kiss. It was a tender kiss. A kiss filled with respect and admiration. She placed her face back against his chest and they held each other tightly. Neither said a word as they embraced.

She lifted her face to his, and as they kissed, she felt tears forming. Soon her tears were running down her cheeks, wetting their lips. Again, she pulled away and pressed her face against his chest. She tried to control her emotion but, as usual, found it impossible. Gary put his cheek against her hair and tightened his embrace as she wept against his chest. She wanted to tell him that for the last several weeks, she knew she loved him, but words were difficult. Her tears expressed her love.

He eased his fingers through her hair and caressed her head against his chest. He held her like that for a few moments, then slowly moved his hand to her cheek and gently lifted her face from his chest. They looked at each other and smiled. He kissed the tears on each cheek, then gently kissed her wet trembling lips. They held each other until they heard Kenny fussing.

Without lifting her head from Gary's chest, she said, "He probably kicked off his blanket and is getting cold."

"Yes. I think you're right. I'll get his stuff and put it in the car while you get him. Then I'll come back for the other things and lock the boat."

Except for talking to Kenny, an occasional comment about how beautiful the day had been, and how *Remedy* had sailed, the ride home was very quiet. They smiled each time they made eye contact and their eyes lingered longer than usual.

⌒

By the time they arrived home, it was dark. Kenny hadn't eaten, and it was past his bedtime. Angie prepared Kenny's dinner while Gary unloaded the car. When Kenny finished eating, Angie gave him his bath and put him to bed. While Angie was getting Kenny to sleep, Gary took a shower. Kenny was tired and sleepy, so it didn't take long before he was asleep. Angie started her shower before Gary finished his. After drying off, she noticed that she was extremely nervous, so nervous she could hardly get her pajamas on.

He was standing at the bar with his back to her. She put her arms around him and kissed his neck.

"Hi, luv," he said.

"Hi."

He turned around; he was holding two full glasses. He handed one to her. "I mixed us a drink."

"A margarita," she said as she licked some of the salt from the rim.

"Yes. Do you like them?"

"I don't know. I've never had one."

"Have you ever had a mixed drink?"

"No, I haven't. But I have a feeling I'm going to." She lifted her glass to his. "To us," she said when their glasses touched. She took a sip. "Wow! This is really good." She took another sip. "Why aren't you drinking your regular gin and grapefruit juice?"

"I thought you'd prefer this."

Angie noticed that he seemed to be as nervous as she. She watched him fidget with his drink, taking a few deep breaths and a few long sips. Without saying anything, he went to his stereo and selected his favorite music. He listened until he was comfortable that what he chose was appropriate, then returned to Angie at the bar. By the look in his eyes, she knew he was going to kiss her. She set her drink on the bar; she was tense but felt certain her eyes reflected her desire. His kiss was more gentle than she expected. She realized that he didn't want to be aggressive and come across as taking advantage of her situation.

He has to be wondering if I would be offended if he were to make a serious pass at me. There's no way I can be misreading his looks, the drinks, and his kisses. There just isn't. He made the first move. Now it's my turn.

He moved away from her and finished his drink. He looked at hers and saw that it was almost empty. "How about another?"

"I'm not sure."

"Don't you like it?"

"Oh, yes! I like it a lot. I'm just not sure I can handle another. I'm starting to feel this one."

"What you need is something to eat. You haven't had anything since lunch." He pulled out a chair at the kitchen table. "You sit here while I fix us another drink. Then I'll cook us a grilled cheese sandwich."

"Perfect."

She couldn't take her eyes off him as he stood at the bar, mixing their drinks. She admired how casual he looked with his large shirt that was left out and over his comfortable-looking shorts. His shorts were way too large for his small behind, and his loose-fitting T-shirt didn't hide his large shoulders or small waist. She had lived with him for over a year and had admired his physique many times before, but this time was different—her thoughts were influenced by desire. She began to squirm in her chair.

He finished mixing their drinks and set hers on the table in front of her. She took a sip.

"This one's even better than the last."

He was standing beside her. She looked up when she noticed he was setting his drink beside hers. He leaned down and gently but cautiously kissed her. She wanted to tell him that he wasn't taking advantage of their situation, and it was what she wanted. She almost reached for him and pulled him back to her, but he moved away before she could.

She watched as he struggled to find something to cook their sandwiches in. All of a sudden, she felt hunger, but it wasn't a hunger for food. Her body was yearning with desire. She stood and went to him. His back was toward her. She slowly wrapped her arms around him and pressed her tingling breasts against his back. He stopped what he was doing and stood motionless as she kissed his neck. She was trembling all over, especially her insides. She heard herself say, "Are you sure you want a sandwich?" She didn't plan to say it—it just came out.

When he turned around, Angie realized, by his expression, that he was concerned. She wondered if she had made a mistake by making him aware of her desire. His worried eyes and shy smile made her wish she had been patient and given him time to get comfortable. She figured it had been at least two or three or maybe more years since he last made love. She felt certain, from their earlier conversations, that Susan was the only one he had been with.

He leaned back against the counter and put his arms around her as she put hers around him. He pulled her close. She watched as his parted lips moved closer and closer to hers. It was as if a surge of electricity went through her body when their lips met. And when their tongues touched, her knees felt as if they were going to buckle. Her breathing was quick and short, and her body trembled as he eased his hand under her pajama top and caressed her breasts. She was no longer concerned.

He pulled away, and they began walking arm in arm toward his bedroom. They were almost to the door when they both and, at the same time, stopped.

"I can't do this," Angie said. "Not in Susan's bed."

"Neither can I."

Angie turned, took his hand, then led him into her bedroom. As soon as they were in her room, they kissed and embraced passionately. They couldn't let go long enough to remove their clothes, so they helped each other. They were very quiet—it was difficult, but they didn't want to wake Kenny. While holding each other, as much as they could, they lay on the bed, on top of the spread. Pulling a bedspread back was not on their minds.

Gary kissed her nipples, then with one in his mouth, he removed his hand from her breasts and began slowly moving it down toward her wet area. He had barely touched it when she encouraged him to roll over on her. She was ready and anxious.

He positioned himself and slowly began to move. Angie couldn't hold back her tears. They were not tears of pain, although there was pain, they were tears of pleasure. He continued to move slowly until he was tight against her. She raised her knees, placed her hands on his back below his waist, and pulled him even closer. He was breathing through clenched teeth, and each breath was louder than the last. Neither moved.

She felt her muscles quivering and tightening around him. She had to move. She positioned herself to be flat against him, then lifted to meet him as he pushed against her. He moaned quietly but didn't move as she jerked and tightened around him. The feeling of him getting harder and harder, then throbbing deep inside, caused a surge of pleasure that she had only imagined. She came close once but had never experienced an orgasm.

There is no way I could have ever imagined the incredible feeling I have enjoyed.

Angie woke the next morning with her back to Gary. His arm was around her with his hand holding her left breast. They were cuddled as close as possible. She knew he was awake from the way he was caressing her breast. She arched her back, forcing her rear against him—he was erect. She turned over and faced him; she was looking forward to their first morning together. He was positioned to kiss her breasts when Kenny began to fuss. He lay back on his pillow.

"Well, he took care of that," Angie said as they looked at each other and smiled

While Angie cared for Kenny, Gary went into his bathroom and took a shower. Angie joined him in his bedroom as he was dressing for work. She came up behind him while he was looking in the mirror, fixing his necktie. She put her arms around him, looked over his shoulder, and said, "Not a bad reflection."

He continued tying his tie. "Not bad at all."

She looked over at his bed. "Will you be sleeping in here?"

He turned around, put his arms around her waist, and said, "I don't know. Should I?"

"You know what I want."

"What do you want?"

"I want you to sleep with me."

"And I want to sleep with you." He kissed her lightly on the lips, then turned and looked at his bed. "I guess we'll have to fix up the third bedroom."

Angie was smiling when he turned back to her. She pulled away a little and said, "I love you so much."

"I love you too. I've known for several months that I love you, but I didn't have the nerve to tell you. I guess I should've told you sooner."

"You chose the perfect time. I also have known I love you, but because of my respect for Susan and thinking you were still grieving for her, I resisted giving in to my feelings. And then there's the biggie I had to deal with—I'm fifteen years younger than you. I'm not even old enough to legally drink. Doesn't that concern you?"

"Not at all. Your mature looks and mind are definitely not that of a nineteen-year-old. I hope you don't think I'm too old for you."

"You sure as hell weren't too old for me last night."

"Thanks. I needed that."

"You needed the compliment, or you needed the sex?"

"Both," he said while laughing. "But I was referring to the compliment."

She had told him, during some of their late-night conversations, about Bob and how he only thought of himself, and the one time with Skip, so he knew he didn't have a tough act to follow.

She kissed him. "You have no idea how much I enjoyed being with you last night. Waves of muscle spasms are rushing down my belly, and I'm getting all juicy just thinking about it."

"Hold that thought until tonight."

She reached for his tie. "You can be late, just this once. Please."

"No, Angie. I can't. And besides, where's Kenny? Where is he?"

"He's in his crib, dry and full, playing with his toys."

"But…"

"There's the sofa or even the floor," she said while pulling his tie. "The carpet's soft."

"The sofa."

CHAPTER 20

Angie was amazed at how Gary found that he didn't need to work as late as before. It wasn't just Tuesdays and Thursdays he came home early; it was almost every night. She always had a nice dinner prepared, and when he arrived, his favorite drink was handed to him at the door. They enjoyed a drink together, ate early, and made love late. They never tired of the routine. Angie was very creative—and not only with her meals.

They mostly enjoyed making love on board *Remedy*. But they never missed an opportunity to make love some place new. All that was required was that they couldn't be seen, or if they were, no one could tell what they were doing. The challenge of making love—in one way or another—and keeping an eye on Kenny, so he wouldn't catch them was always exciting. Many times they had commented about how the last time was their best. Angie figured that if they were sincere in their belief, that the last was the best, they would always look forward to the next "last time."

It was two weeks before Christmas. Angie and Gary were standing on the dock, looking at his finished home. They had just returned from a day of excellent sailing and great sex. The next day, Monday, he would get his certificate of occupancy. And Tuesday, Ruby and Carl were going to help them move.

Gary was holding Kenny with his left arm and Angie with his other. Kenny had started walking, so they couldn't leave him on the boat or put him down. It was a cool evening, and they were snuggled close. Angie felt his arm tighten around her as he asked, "What do you want for Christmas?"

"I don't know. What do you want?"

"You."

"You get me almost every day. What else?"

"I want you forever."

"What do you mean?"

"I want to marry you. Will you marry me?"

She put her arms around him and Kenny. "Yes. Definitely, yes. I love you more than you can imagine, and there's nothing that could make me happier."

Still holding them, she forced her face hard against Gary's chest. His shirt absorbed her tears as she shook with emotion. She heard Kenny whimpering; he didn't understand. She looked at him and saw his little chin quivering. She took him in her arms. "It's okay. Mommy's not hurt. I'm crying because I'm happy." After drying her eyes, she said, "I wish I could control my tears. I'm just a big crybaby."

"That's one of the reasons I love you. You can't hide your feelings."

⌒〜⌒

By the end of the week, Angie, Gary, and Kenny were settled in their new home. Angie contacted Rev. Buchanan. He was pleased that she had chosen him to perform the ceremony. Angie wanted to be married on Christmas Day, but Rev. Buchanan was too busy that day, so they agreed on December 23.

They were married in their new home, and like Ruby, Angie kept her wedding small. Ruby, Carl, Gayle, Wayne, and Rev. Buchanan's wife were the only ones there.

⌒〜⌒

On Christmas day, Angie and Gary were sitting on the floor in front of the Christmas tree, helping Kenny open his presents.

The excitement of getting married and organizing their home had left them with little time to buy gifts, so most of the presents were Kenny's. When Angie picked up her last gift, she noticed an envelope under it. ANGIE, in bold letters, was the only word on it. She opened the present first, then burst into tears when she opened the envelope.

Still holding the card, she threw her arms around Gary and began crying uncontrollably.

"Oh, Gary," she wailed. "I love you."

He was sitting with his legs straight out in front, with his arms behind him for support. When Angie put her arms around him and he put his around her, he was forced backward. They held each other tightly as he slowly fell to the floor; they continued their embrace as she lay on his chest and cried.

Gary waited until her crying had subsided enough to answer. "Well?" he asked.

She lifted her face to his and felt her lips trembling as they kissed. "You know the answer. Of course you can. There's nothing I want more. You've made this the happiest day of my life." She tried, without success, to gain control of her emotions; there was much she wanted to say.

Kenny became concerned and went to his mother. She felt him touching her back. While still crying, she rose off Gary and lifted her baby in her arms. She caressed him against her chest, put her wet cheek on his little head, and said, "Guess what, Kenny? You have a father."

With Kenny still in her arms, she read the card again:

> I love you, Angie.
>
> I also love your son.
>
> Would you mind if I adopt him?

With one arm around her baby and the other around her husband, she said, "Thanks." She tried, but that's all she could say.

Angie

The layout of their new home was excellent; they had no regrets with the design or the decisions they made. Angie never tired of standing on their back deck, looking down at the clear water in their large pool, listening to the seagulls, and admiring *Remedy* resting comfortably at its dock. The evenings were enjoyed most. That's when she and Gary relaxed on the deck with a glass of wine or mixed drink and listened to the romantic sounds of the night. Even though they were not on the Gulf, they were close enough to hear the waves breaking against the shore.

Occasionally, on the nights Gary came home early, they would take Kenny to the beach and walk in the surf. Kenny never tried to pull his hands from his mother or father as he walked between them, splashing and kicking the water with his feet. He loved attention and being close.

Kenny looked forward to weekends just as much as his mom and dad; that's when they went sailing aboard *Remedy*. Mostly, they sailed in Sarasota Bay, but when they had time and the weather was favorable, they sailed in the Gulf or Tampa Bay. After Kenny's second birthday, they became more comfortable with taking longer trips and staying overnight. Their favorite place to anchor overnight was on Egmont Key. Kenny enjoyed playing in the calm water along the beach and going inland to find and watch the many gopher tortoises that inhabit the island. Both Kenny and his parents never tired of exploring the old gun emplacements that were built during the Spanish-American War and the houses and streets of old Fort Dade.

They preferred sailing in Tampa Bay where the larger, faster boats sailed. Angie would scan the bay for a boat that looked like a worthy opponent. When she found one, she steered *Remedy* toward it while Gary trimmed the sails. It never took long before *Remedy* would overtake the other boat and pass it. Then she'd search for another.

Angie was about to pass a slower victim when she glanced aft. There was a boat approaching fast.

"Gary!" she yelled. "Look what's behind us!"

"Oh my god! Look at that beauty. And she's gaining fast. Maybe we can outsail her if we're closer to the wind."

Angie chose a new course; Gary trimmed the sails.

Not believing what was happening, Angie shouted, "She's still gaining on us."

"Let's fall off the wind and see if that helps."

Angie changed course and Gary adjusted the sails. The other boat also changed course. Angie kept her eyes on the direction of the wind and held her course. Soon, it was obvious: they were going to be overtaken.

"Can you believe how fast she's coming up on us?" Angie said.

Gary shook his head in disbelief. "No. I can't. I wonder what make she is?" They didn't have long to wait before his question was answered.

As the other boat sped by, with all aboard smiling and waving, he looked at the mainsail: M38. "That's a Morgan 38. I heard they were fast, but I had no idea they were that fast."

Painted on the transom and in large bold letters was its name, *Tooler*, and below the name, St. Petersburg, Florida. Gary and Angie said the name at the same time, "Tooler." They watched without talking as *Tooler* sailed ahead of *Remedy*, increasing its lead.

"I think a Morgan 38 should be our next boat," Angie said.

"As soon as we can afford one."

A few days after Kenny started the first grade, he asked his mother if she would start calling him Ken.

"Why?" she asked.

"Ken sounds more mature."

She smiled when she heard him use the word "mature." She realized he was no longer her baby. "Sure. From now on, except when I forget, your dad and I will call you Ken."

"Thanks, Mom."

"Can I have one last hug while you're still Kenny and not too mature to hug?"

He put his arms around her. "I'll never be too mature to hug."

She hugged him again, then wiped the tears from her eyes as he walked away.

Angie found that while Ken was in school, she had a lot of extra time. She took advantage of the time by going to real estate classes. After passing her test, she began working for a real estate office on Longboat Key, not far from her home. She hadn't worked long when a nice home on a canal in Bradenton came on the market. The price was extremely reasonable. When she went to look at the house, she visualized it as the perfect home for Ruby and Carl. She rushed to her husband's restaurant, where they worked, and told them they had to get off work and look at this house; it wouldn't be on the market long. Carl could leave, but Ruby had too many tables she was responsible for.

Carl checked out the house, then Angie encouraged him to walk out on the dock with her. She saw in his eyes the desire to own it and wanted to get him away from the owners. Angie turned around to look at the canal; Carl turned with her. She pretended to be showing him the dock and canal.

"Your excitement is starting to show," she said. "Don't let the owners see it."

"I know I should act as if I'm not all that interested, but, Angie, this is the perfect house for Ruby and me."

"I know."

"What should I do?"

"Make them an offer."

"Make them an offer! My god, Angie, the price is already so low, I'm afraid someone will buy it before Ruby can see it."

"That's the reason I want you to make an offer. If we rush back to my office and put a contract together with your offer, then I can return here with a signed contract. No one else can buy it until the negotiations are finished. They probably won't accept your offer, but they can counter. That will give Ruby a chance to look at the house and time to make sure it's what you and she want."

"How much should we offer?"

"As much as I'd like to tell you, I can't. But I will lower my commission to as low as I'm allowed."

Carl said a figure. Angie looked down at the dock. He said a lower one. She raised her eyes to his. "Let's go sign a contract."

Later that day, Angie called Carl. "I hope Ruby likes her new home."

"She will. We're going to look at it in a little while." He paused for a moment to let what she said register. "What're you telling me?"

"They accepted your offer."

"You have to be kidding!"

"I'm not kidding. Can you believe it?"

"I can't! It's like I'm dreaming. Thank you, Angie. Thank you so much. I have to tell Ruby. Bye."

Not only did Ruby and Carl love their new home, everything worked out well for Angie. When Ruby and Carl moved out of her house, the house her grandmother left her, and into their new home, Gayle and her fiancé moved in. Angie left the rent the same as Ruby and Carl paid. By paying low rent for seven years was one of the reasons Ruby and Carl were able to save enough money for the down payment for their new home. Now Angie wanted to help Gayle and her fiancé do the same.

In less than a year, Angie, or Angela as all but her close friends called her, became a prosperous realtor. Mostly, she sold homes and property on Longboat Key, but occasionally, she sold in Bradenton and Sarasota. Even though she worked hard and loved her work, she still went home early to be there when Ken arrived from school. Her hours were less than most, but her sales were high. Because of her clients' trust and respect, they recommended her to their friends. The other real estate offices admired the ethical manner in which she dealt with their clients; not only did they trust her, they enjoyed working with her.

Angie

After a little over a year of working for a real estate office, she got her broker's license. But she knew that before she could open her own office, she had to have help. Especially with the hours she kept. A real estate office that closed at 3:30 wasn't practical. She wanted someone she could trust, and that excluded her colleagues. The only two people she knew that she trusted completely were Ruby and Gayle. She felt certain that Ruby's energy and personality combined with Gayle's ability to run an office had to be a winning combination. Gayle was already working as a receptionist and secretary for a real estate office in Sarasota.

When Angie mentioned her plan to open her own office to Ruby and Gayle, they were thrilled that she wanted them to work with her and eagerly signed up for the next real estate class. The location Angie chose for her business was on Longboat Key, not far from her home. It was a new building, close to being finished, and by the time the offices were furnished, Ruby and Gayle had their licenses.

Angie would never forget that first day. They were arranging the furniture and getting organized when a man came in and said he had the sign ready. She asked him to install it on the building where she had shown him earlier.

Soon, they heard the man say, "It's up."

Angie turned to Ruby and Gayle. "Let's go take a look at our sign."

As they walked out, Ruby said, "You never told us what you were going to name your business. What did you name it?"

By then, they were in the parking area, in front of the building. Angie turned around, and they turned with her. They felt a special bond and had a group hug when they read the sign: "Best Friends Real Estate." Ruby and Gayle realized how close they were, but now Angie was informing the community.

Ruby and Gayle caught on quickly to the real estate business. Their sales were many, and it wasn't long before they were as well-known as Angie. In only a few months, the business was showing a profit, and all were taking home large checks.

CHAPTER 21

It was early on a Sunday morning when Angie heard Gary shout, "Hot damn! Angie, come look at this."

She stopped preparing the food for the cruise they planned to take later that morning. He was reading the Sunday paper. His face expressed his excitement as he pointed to an ad in the classified section. Angie knelt down beside him and read the ad: Morgan 38, in excellent condition. She didn't read the rest of the ad.

"It's not too early," she said. "Let's call."

"Are you sure it's not too early?"

"Come on, Gary. Call before someone else does."

"I don't know. I hate to call someone this early, especially on a Sunday morning."

"Seven isn't that early." She stood and reached for his hand and began pulling him out of his chair. "Come on, hon. Please call. I'd call, but I don't know the questions to ask."

"Okay. I'll call."

Angie stood by Gary and listened as he talked to the owner. Her excitement increased when she saw him write the owner's address—she knew they were going to see the boat.

When Gary finished talking with the owner, he shouted, "Stop what you're doing! We have to hurry. Where's Ken?"

"He's getting dressed to go sailing."

"The boat is in Saint Petersburg. The owner said that someone is going to be looking at it when they get out of church, so we have to get there before church lets out. Let's hurry."

Angie rushed to Ken's room. "Hurry and get dressed. We have to go to St. Pete and look at a Morgan 38."

"A Morgan 38! Really?"

"Yes, really. So hurry."

"What about breakfast?"

"We'll eat something later. We have to get there before someone else does."

"I'll hurry."

Even though Ken was only eight, he was just as anxious. He had watched *Tooler* sailing in Tampa Bay many times and had admired her looks and experienced her speed.

The owner's ad was right. The boat was in excellent condition. The owner bought it new, and it was obvious that he had given it a lot of tender loving care. Gary and Angie asked him many questions before asking the price. The price was reasonable, and when they tried to get him to lower it a little, he refused to negotiate. He knew what he had and had it priced accordingly. Angie and Gary's eyes spoke to each other; they had to have her.

The owner said, "I'd like to take you sailing, but I told the other people that if they got here around one o'clock, I'd take them."

Angie asked, "Do they have first refusal?"

"No, they don't. I just told them if they like the boat and want to take a test sail, I would take them. And if after sailing on her, they aren't interested and you want to try her out, I can take you sailing next weekend."

Gary looked at Angie, then back at the owner. "We have heard a lot about the Morgan 38 and have seen one in action, so we won't need a demonstration. And you won't need to take the other people out this afternoon. Will you take a personal check for a deposit?"

"A personal check will be fine."

"I'll bring a cashier's check for the balance when we pick her up. Can we leave her here until next weekend? We have to find a home for our other boat."

"You can leave her here as long as you like. I hate to see her go."

On the way home, they stopped to get something to eat, but their stomachs were so knotted with excitement that after ordering, they just sat and looked at their food.

"What are we going to do with *Remedy*?" Ken asked.

His dad answered, "Maybe until we can sell her, Carl and Ruby will let us keep her at their dock?"

Angie thought for a moment. "And maybe they'd like to buy her."

"Maybe," Gary said as he moved his food with his fork. He stopped moving his food. "I know one thing for sure."

"What's that?" Angie asked.

"I'm glad you were as persistent as you were that I call—if you hadn't been, we may not own a Morgan 38."

"Thanks."

Gary began playing with his food again. "I have a good idea. Let's name our new boat, *Persistence*. What do you think?"

"I like it."

"Why would you want to change her name?" Ken asked.

Angie looked at Gary for a moment, then back to Ken. "Do you mean...?"

"Yep. She's *Tooler*."

Gary shook his head. "I can't believe I checked her out from stem to stern without seeing the name."

"I can't believe I didn't notice it either. I guess it was because the dock was short and the transom was beyond the end."

"Well," Ken said, "I had to know. So I leaned over the aft rail and looked."

Ken had started eating and was almost finished. Gary and Angie were still too excited to enjoy their food and were slowly eating. Angie put her fork down. "If we hurry, we can stop by Carl and Ruby's on the way home and see if it's all right with them to leave *Remedy* at their dock. And if so, we will still have time to move her this afternoon."

Gary dropped his fork and picked up the check. "Let's go."

The next morning at work, Ruby was beaming with delight when she approached Angie. "*Remedy* looks so good tied to our dock that we've decided to buy her."

"Great! I'd hate to see her leave the family."

"The price you quoted sounds more than fair to us. I'll go to the bank today and start the financing procedure."

"No hurry."

Ruby and Carl had sailed aboard *Remedy* many times and were familiar with how she sailed and how to sail her. There was no need for instructions.

Ruby joined Gary, Ken, and Angie when they went to get *Tooler*; Carl had to work. So to return their car, Gayle and her fiancé followed in their car; Gayle would drive it back.

It was a perfect day for sailing, clear, with a moderate breeze. Angie was at her normal location: the helm. She was accustomed to steering with a tiller but found it easy to adapt to *Tooler's* large wheel. While crossing Tampa Bay and jockeying through a series of maneuvers, she became more familiar with their new boat and was impressed with how easy it handled. *Tooler* was no more difficult to sail than *Remedy* and much faster. She had worried all night if she would be able to handle a larger boat.

The wind had slowed by the time they reached the south side of Tampa Bay. Except for the few times Gary took the wheel and when she encouraged Ken and Ruby to give it a try, Angie had been at the helm most of the way. Ruby and Ken were sitting on the front deck, with their backs against the cabin when Angie turned into the narrow twisting channel that lead to Sarasota Bay.

As Angie maneuvered from one channel marker to the next, she observed a small sailboat coming toward her. She held to her side, close to the markers, giving it plenty of room to pass. It was a good-looking little boat and well maintained.

When the boat was beside her, as is the custom, she waved at the man and woman and a boy about the size of Ken. The man gave her the thumbs-up sign; the others returned her wave.

She looked ahead to make sure she was in the channel as their boats passed. The boat was behind her when she glanced at it again. She gasped and felt a sharp pain in her belly. The name painted on the transom had almost buckled her knees. It was *Fate*. She wondered if Skip had sold his boat—or was that Skip. She continued to look at the little boat until she heard Gary say, "You're getting out of the channel, hon." She quickly put *Tooler* back on course and never looked back.

She knew the picture of the boat with the three people in it and the man holding his thumb in the air would always be with her. She also realized how little it affected her. After that first shock, when she read the name, she had regained her composure and put it out of her mind. She didn't care if it was Skip or not and definitely didn't want to find out that it was and complicate her life.

Tooler turned out to be the perfect boat. Almost every weekend, they could be seen sailing either in Sarasota Bay, Tampa Bay, or out in the Gulf. Occasionally, they sailed to a calm anchorage and stayed overnight. When they had a three- or four-day weekend, they sailed to Boca Grande. When Carl and Gary had the same days off, they took both *Remedy* and *Tooler* out together. More often than not, Gayle and her fiancé, Mark, joined them. Gayle and Mark loved sailing as much as the others and were welcomed on either boat— even on the overnight cruises.

During the summer, when Ken was out of school and Gary could take two or more weeks off, they sailed to the Keys. They always sailed alone: Carl stayed to manage the restaurant; Ruby and Gayle managed the real estate office.

They survived many storms without a serious problem. Gary had *Tooler* rigged for single-handed sailing and could sail her alone if he had to, but never did. Neither Angie, Gary, nor Ken feared bad weather. They actually looked forward to the test. They thought ahead of the storm and always had the right jib on and the main reefed properly before the storm hit. Because they couldn't see the storms at night, they rarely sailed with full sail.

"With a boat this size and only three to handle her," Gary had cautioned, "it's better to have too little sail than too much."

CHAPTER 22

Gary had called earlier to say he was on his way home. It was December 23, their tenth wedding anniversary. She had their drink glasses on the bar, ready for their favorite drink to be mixed as soon as she saw him pull in the driveway or heard the garage door opening. The table was set, the potatoes were ready to be placed in the oven, the salad was fixed, and in the refrigerator, the steaks were on the counter waiting for Gary's magic seasoning and superb grilling, the wine in a decanter, the candles ready to be lit.

Ken finished his shower, then joined his mother at the stereo to help select some appropriate music. They were listening to and talking about some of the music they chose when Angie looked at her watch. "I wonder where your dad is? He called over an hour ago and said he was leaving. He's never late."

"He probably forgot to get you a present for your anniversary and stopped to buy you something."

"You're probably right."

They left the stereo and began tinkering with the lights and ornaments on the Christmas tree.

Ken looked down at the many presents. "Did you get me and Dad the baseball gloves we picked out?"

"I can't tell you. You'll have to wait until we open our presents Christmas morning."

He picked up a large present and read the names, "To Ken and Dad. I bet they're in here."

Angie tried to not smile. "I doubt it."

"Yeah, right."

Angie looked at the clock on the mantle. "It sure is taking him a long time to find me something, if that's what he's doing. Let's go sit on the deck while we're waiting."

They reminisced about many of their adventures, then discussed their plans for future adventures. After a while, Ken said, "I'm getting cold. I think we should go in."

"I agree." Angie glanced at the clock on the stove. "Wow! It's been more than two hours since he called. I wonder what he's up to? Do you think I should call the restaurant and see if he got delayed?"

"Maybe."

"I'll wait a few more minutes."

She heard a car pull in the drive. She rushed to their drink glasses, picked them up, and was getting ready to put ice in them when she realized she didn't hear the garage door open. She put the glasses back on the bar. She and Ken glanced at each other, then went to the window to see who it was. Two deputies were getting out of their car. Angie's heart felt as if it stopped, then felt as if it were going to beat out of her chest. She knew something had happened to Gary. She put her arm around Ken and opened the door.

"Are you Angela Martin?"

"Yes."

"Can we come in?"

She didn't answer. With her arm around Ken, they stepped back and let the deputies in.

The deputy who was doing the talking had prepared what he had to say so he could get it said quickly before Angie began asking questions.

"I'm sorry, but I have some bad news. Your husband swerved to miss an elderly lady walking in the road and hit a large power pole. He was killed instantly."

The other deputy had positioned himself so he could assist her if she fainted. It was a good thing he did. She didn't faint, but her legs became so weak they couldn't support her. He held her up and helped her to a chair. Ken joined his mother in the chair. Tears filled the deputies' eyes as they watched Ken and his mother holding each other and crying loudly.

One of the deputies cleared his throat and asked, "Is there someone I can call?"

Angie pointed to a small black book by the phone. He brought it to her. She opened it and pointed to two names. He continuously cleared his throat as he talked on the phone. He informed Ruby, then Gayle of what happened, then returned to Angie and Ken.

"They'll be right over. We'll stay with you until they arrive."

She motioned for them to have a seat. They sat on the sofa without talking. After a few minutes, Angie asked, "Where is he?"

"He's at Blake Hospital. You'll need to let them know what funeral home to call."

"I'll let Rev. Buchanan take care of that."

"Would you like me to call him?"

"Yes, please. His number is in the same book."

He called, then returned to the sofa. "He's coming to be with you."

"Thanks."

The front door flew open, and Ruby rushed in, crying uncontrollably. She leaned down beside the chair Angie and Ken were in, put her arms around them, and cried with even more emotion. Gayle was also crying uncontrollably when she and Mark arrived. Ruby moved away from Angie and Ken enough to allow Gayle to get her arms around them.

The deputies shook Mark's hand and introduced themselves. Mark asked some questions about the accident. They told him an elderly lady had walked in front of Gary's car and how he had chosen to hit a pole rather than her or the oncoming traffic. They gave their condolences and left.

Carl arrived soon after; Mark explained what happened.

Carl had worked for Gary since he was in high school and was having a difficult time controlling his emotions. He finally eased between Ruby and Gayle. He wanted to say something to Angie and Ken, but when he looked into their eyes, he couldn't speak. He broke down and cried with them.

When Rev. Buchanan arrived, everyone moved away from Angie and Ken. Angie heard him talking and knew he was trying to comfort her but couldn't make out his words. It was like she was having a bad dream and what was happening would be over when she woke. Reality was sudden when she heard him say something about funeral arrangements.

"No funeral," she cried. "Many times, Gary and I have talked about what to do. And we both want the same. He wants to be taken straight to the crematorium without a funeral or memorial service of any kind. He wants a minimal mention of his death in the paper, and he wants no flowers." By saying "what he wants" instead of "what he wanted," everyone realized that she had not accepted his death. They understood.

"I'll make sure everything is performed as Gary wished," Rev. Buchanan said. He stayed a little longer, comforting Angie and Ken. "I better go. I need to start making things happen. I'll stop at the hospital on my way home."

Ruby and Gayle cried as hard as they had earlier when they took the dishes and wine glasses off the table. They continued to cry as they put the bread in its container and the steak back in the refrigerator. Ruby managed to say, "What a wonderful anniversary this would've been."

"But instead…" Gayle couldn't finish.

They hugged and lost what little control they had.

Ruby and Gayle stayed with Angie and Ken that night. They stayed up late talking and reminiscing. After listening to Ruby, Gayle, and his mom talking about their experiences, Ken understood why they were such close friends and respected them even more. When they could hardly hold their eyes open, they agreed to try and get some sleep. Ken had already fallen asleep. Ruby and Gayle wanted to sleep with Angie, but that's where Ken slept.

Angie was up first, had a pot of coffee made, and was sitting at the kitchen table having a cup when Ruby and Gayle joined her.

"This is one helluva Christmas," Angie said as she got up to pour them a cup of coffee. "I don't know what I'd do without you.

193

Besides Ken, you're the only family I have. How in the hell will Ken and I get through this?"

Ruby lifted her cup, took a sip, and said, "Like you have every other catastrophe in your life. With courage and determination."

"But this catastrophe is larger than the others."

"I know it's big. It's humongous. But with our help, you'll make it."

"You'll make it," Gayle added. "And we'll do everything we can to make life tolerable. Speaking of helping, what are we going to do tomorrow?"

Angie put her face in her hands. "I wish I could just go away and return when it's over."

Gayle put her hand on Angie's. "Now, Angie. Think of what Gary wants you to do. Visualize him looking down at you, which he is. He wouldn't want you to run off and hide. He'd want you and Ken to enjoy this Christmas as much as possible."

"I know. What do you suggest?"

"I think we should start cooking the pies, cakes, and cookies this afternoon. Tomorrow, we can cook the turkey and the rest of the Christmas dinner. Just like we did when your grandmother had her stroke."

"I don't know. That sounds a little too festive to me."

"Come on, Angie. Gayle's right. If it were just you, I'd go off and hide with you. But we have to think of Ken."

"You're right, guys. Let's try to make the day as much like Christmas as possible."

Gayle found some paper and a pencil. "Okay. What do we need from the store?"

Ruby and Gayle made sure that Angie and Ken were never left alone; one or both were always with them. Later that day, Rev. Buchanan dropped by with some papers for Angie to sign. She thanked him for giving up some of his Christmas. Ruby gave him a pie and some cookies to take home.

Angie

Soon after Rev. Buchanan left, Angie joined Ruby and Gayle on the deck. Angie broke the silence, "You know? It seems that everyone I've loved has either died or deceived me. My dad died in an automobile accident, my mother died in a fire, my grandmother, and now Gary. You know what Bob and Skip did. I'll never love again."

"I wouldn't rule love out," Ruby said.

"You never know what will happen," Gayle added. "Time heals all."

"I don't think so," Angie sighed. "Not this time."

⌒

Angie was awake, watching her son as he slept beside her. When he opened his eyes, he was looking into hers. She put her arm across his chest, kissed him on the forehead, and said, "Merry Christmas."

"Merry Christmas. But it's really not too merry, is it?"

"No, it's not. But since Ruby and Gayle are trying hard to cheer us up, we shouldn't let them down. So let's open our presents and try not to get emotional. Remember, your dad is watching, and it will disturb him to see us not enjoying Christmas."

"Mom?"

"Yes."

"Are baseball gloves in that present?"

"Yes."

"Would you mind if before Ruby and Gayle get up, I get the present and put it in my room? I'd like to open it later."

"I understand."

Ken eased out of bed, but before he left the room, he turned and looked back at his mother. "Is there any that you'd like me to bring back for you?"

"Yes, there is. The one that says, 'To Dad, From Mom.' And the one that says, 'To Mom, From Dad.' I'll open mine later too." Angie was thankful that she and Gary had agreed to buy each other only one gift.

⌒

Christmas dinner was excellent, the desserts were delicious, and by the end of the day, Angie and Ken were feeling comfortable enough to join in the laughter. Angie felt the day went well, a lot better than she had expected. Ruby stayed with them that night and Gayle the next. After that, they were on their own.

On Friday of the following week, Rev. Buchanan delivered Gary's ashes to Angie.

Gary had requested his ashes be spread in the gulf. Ruby had called earlier and suggested that Ken and she join Carl, Gayle, Mark, and her aboard *Remedy* to spread the ashes. Angie agreed.

Carl headed *Remedy* out Longboat Pass and into the gulf. It was the last weekend of Christmas vacation; Ken would return to school on Monday. The weather was fair and the seas were calm. Mark trimmed the sails, and to stay warm, Ruby and Gayle went below. Angie and Ken shared a blanket and were cuddled close together in the cockpit; Ken seldom took his eyes off the box in his mother's lap. No one talked.

Carl sailed straight out, and when he was about two miles offshore, he pulled just off the wind. Without saying a word, everyone knew he had chosen the location. The only sounds aboard *Remedy* were the sails as they occasionally luffed from being close to the wind. Ruby and Gayle joined the others in the cockpit; Mark held the tiller. Angie and Ken were holding the box with Gary's ashes.

She could no longer hold back her tears as she shook with emotion and began to cry.

"I love you, hon," she managed to say. "And always will."

Ken's hand was on top of the box when his mother reluctantly handed it to Carl. Ken looked at his and his mother's tears on the box and the back of his hand as the box slowly left his mother's hands, then his.

"Goodbye Dad," he said as it slid from his fingers.

Carl was standing on the deck, next to the cockpit, and leaning against the lifelines. He was about to lift the lid when

Angie remembered what Wayne had said when she was laying her grandmother to rest.

"Carl," she whispered. "Get close to the water before you open it. That way, the wind won't blow the ashes back in your face."

"Thanks. I'm glad you thought of that." He knelt on the deck, and with both hands holding the box, he leaned as far over the side as he could, took the lid off, then poured the ashes on the water. No one but Carl watched the ashes as they slowly disappeared below the surface.

When Carl headed toward home, Angie took her son's hand and walked forward. They sat on the deck and leaned back against the front of the cabin. They didn't talk; they just held hands and absorbed the memory of the day. It was a closure of sort, and now they had to get on with their lives.

Angie promoted Carl to manager of the restaurant. He had been the assistant manager for several years. With Carl relieving her from the stress of operating a restaurant, she was able to concentrate on her real estate business. She, along with Ruby and Gayle, became extremely successful and envied by other agents. They were affectionately referred to as "The Girls."

It wasn't easy, but Angie and Ken made it through the first year, Christmas being the most difficult. They had taken *Tooler* out several times during that year and two times at the beginning of the second. They tried to pick days that were clear with little wind. The few times they ventured out into the gulf or Tampa Bay, Gayle and Mark had joined them. But now that Gayle was pregnant and close to having her baby, she was reluctant to go. Angie and Ken had not been comfortable when they took *Tooler* out alone; they realized if they were caught in a squall, *Tooler* would be more than they could handle. Ken suggested they sell her and get a smaller boat.

CHAPTER 23

"Mom!" Ken yelled. "Someone's here to look at *Tooler*."
Angie called from the kitchen, "I'll be right there."
She was heating water for tea, and after turning off
the stove, she entered the living room. A man and a young boy, she
assumed was his son, were standing inside the front door. She offered
her hand.

"Hi, I'm Angela. Are you the man who called earlier?"

"Yes. I'm Harvey, and this is my son, Rick."

"Hi, Rick. And this is my son, Ken." Ken shook hands with
Rick, then Harvey. Even though Harvey had said only a few words,
his voice was familiar. Angie was wondering where she remembered
him from. "The boat is in the back," she said. "Instead of walking
around the house, let's go out the back door."

Harvey seemed reluctant to walk across her carpet. "Our shoes
may have dirt on them. We don't mind walking around."

"You'll be fine. Ken, will you take Harvey and Rick to see *Tooler*
while I finish making tea? I'll be out as soon as I finish."

"Sure."

Angie studied Harvey as he walked away. She couldn't place
him. She turned on the stove, then stood at the sink and looked out
the window at Harvey and his son. They were standing on the dock
looking at *Tooler*.

*Maybe his beard is new, and that's why I'm not able to recognize
him.*

Normally, she didn't like beards, but his was short and well-
kept. She thought how it definitely didn't take away from his good
looks—if anything, his tough appearance was enhanced by it.

As she stared out the window, trying to remember where she had heard his voice and seen his familiar eyes, her thoughts were interrupted by the sound of water boiling. She quickly turned the stove off and finished the tea.

$$\backsim$$

"What do you think?" Angie asked as she joined them on the dock.

Without looking at Angie, Harvey said, "She's a beauty. I can't believe you're selling her."

"We'd rather not, but she's a little too large for Ken and me to handle."

"You and Ken take her out alone?"

"Yes. But only in fair weather. I'm afraid if we were caught in a storm, we couldn't handle her. My husband rigged her for single-handed sailing, but without him, she's still a little difficult for just the two of us."

"It sounds like your husband is no longer with you."

"He died in an automobile accident a little over a year ago."

"I'm sorry. My wife also died a little over a year ago. She had breast cancer."

"I'm sure you and Rick had some difficult times."

"We did…and still are. That's why we're looking for a larger boat. One we can take on long cruises and get away from the memories. Not that we want to forget her, we want other adventures, different adventures from the ones shared with her, ones we can enjoy without grieving and missing her."

Angie was still trying to recognize his voice and eyes while he talked. *Is he someone who recently came in the office before he grew the beard?* Her curiosity was distracting her, and before it became obvious, she began talking about the boat. "Do you own a boat now?"

"Yes. It's a small one, nothing like this."

"Is *Tooler* the size you're looking for?"

"Exactly. Tell me about her."

"She's a Morgan 38. She's extremely fast and easy to handle. As you can see, she's rigged for single-handed sailing. She has a Perkins diesel engine and many options, including air conditioning. The air conditioner only works when she's tied to a dock with shore power. The AC is on now. Let's go below where it's cool."

They boarded, and Angie opened the companionway door while Ken showed Harvey and Rick the roller furling, the condition of the sails, and answered their questions.

Angie was straightening up below when she heard Harvey say, "It's nice and cool in here." He had joined her in the cabin.

"And look how spacious!" he continued.

She showed and explained the electronics, then she and Harvey went out and sat in the cockpit while Ken showed Rick the cabin. Angie watched them through the companionway as they lay on the berths and talked. She imagined that Ken was telling Rick about the many times he had cruised to the Keys and other islands.

Harvey and Angie sat across from each other in the cockpit; he was evaluating the boat and asking questions; she was evaluating him while answering his questions. He stood behind the wheel, looked forward, and without looking at Angie, asked, "Is the price in the paper firm?"

"Pretty much. But I think before we do any negotiating, you should check out how she sails."

"I'd love to. When can we?"

"Let's see. It's a little late today. Tomorrow is Sunday. Do you go to church?"

"No, we don't."

"What about tomorrow morning?"

"What time?"

"Nine."

"We'll be here. What can I bring?"

"Whatever you and Rick like to drink. I'll fix something to eat. We'll make a day of it, if you don't have other plans."

Harvey called into the cabin. "Hey, Rick. Guess what?"

"I give up."

Angie and Ken smiled when they heard Rick's answer.

Harvey continued, "Angela asked us to go sailing tomorrow."

"Really?"

"Yes, really," Angie answered.

"All right!"

She smiled as the boys high-fived. Angie was still looking at the boys when she said, "It's amazing how close they are in size. What's Rick's age?"

"He's twelve."

"That's Ken's age. What's his birth date?"

"November 25."

"He's three weeks older than Ken. No wonder they're so close in size."

"Mom. Can Rick and I swim in the pool?"

"Sure. If it's okay with his father."

"Can I, Dad?"

Harvey looked at Angie. "Are you sure you don't mind?"

"Not at all."

"You don't have your bathing suit," Harvey said.

"Ken said I could use one of his."

"Have fun."

"We will," they yelled as they ran to the house.

Angie locked the companionway door. "Let's go sit on the deck and watch them swim. We'll talk more about *Tooler* tomorrow."

"You have a beautiful home," Harvey said as he chose a chair.

"Thanks. Can I fix you a drink?"

"Tea?" Harvey asked.

"Not necessarily. Can I get you a beer, or would you prefer a mixed drink?"

"What do you suggest?"

"My favorite drink, on a hot day like today, is gin over crushed ice with a splash of grapefruit juice."

"That sounds perfect."

She returned with their drinks and sat in the chair beside his. They watched their sons swim and admired how well they got along. She didn't ask about his wife and he didn't ask about her husband; they mostly talked about their sons and *Tooler*. When she returned with fresh drinks, he barely acknowledged her presence; he seemed to be in deep thought. Even while sipping his drink, she noticed that he didn't take his eyes off the boys. She wondered what he was thinking.

"Is something wrong?" she asked.

"No. Nothing's wrong." After a few minutes without talking, he said, "I'm sorry…I was just thinking how much they look alike. They could pass for brothers."

"Now that you mentioned it, they do look similar."

He finished his drink, then called to his son, "We better be going."

∽

Later that night while Angie and Ken were having dinner, Ken asked, "Do you think we'll have time tomorrow to anchor at Egmont Key and go ashore?"

"I'm sure we will. Harvey didn't act like they had to hurry home. I guess I better call him and remind him to bring their bathing suits. Oh no! I forgot to get his phone number. And I don't even know his last name."

"Rick told me," Ken said. "It's Chastain."

Angie returned the fork to her plate. A sharp pain gripped her stomach and her hands began to tremble. She tried to take a sip of tea, but her hand was trembling so much she couldn't lift the glass. With her eyes fixed on the food in her plate, she heard Ken ask, "What's wrong, Mom?"

She heard his question but didn't answer.

"Mom, are you all right?"

"I'm fine. I just felt a little lightheaded for a minute. I'm okay now."

"Are you sure?"

It was obvious that Ken was concerned. She faked a smile. "Yes, I'm sure. How about looking their number up and giving them a call while I clean off the table and put the dishes in the dishwasher?"

"Okay."

Her hands were shaking so much, she could hardly rinse the dishes. Ken returned. She cleared her throat to help get her voice started. "Did you get him?"

"The phone book only had two Chastains listed. I tried both, and the people that answered said they don't know Harvey, but they have had a few people call and ask for him."

One of the calls was thirteen years ago. Only I wasn't asking for Harvey.

"Let's hope they think to bring their suits."

While Ken watched television, Angie went out on the deck and sat in her favorite lounge chair. The night was cool, and she could barely hear the television. It was the perfect night for some serious thinking, which she had plenty to do. She wondered if, while Harvey watched the boys swim and he was in that trance-like state, it had dawned on him that thirteen years before, on a rainy night, in a car with the windows steamed up, she was the Angie he had made love to…and that he could be Ken's father.

Angie could not keep from smiling when she thought how, when younger, he preferred to be called Skip. *A name like Harvey probably inspired a lot of teasing.*

Ken joined his mother. He kissed her on the cheek. "Good night, Mom."

"Good night, Kenny. I love you."

"I love you too. But please don't call me Kenny."

"I realize it's selfish of me to call you Kenny, but Ken is such an adult name, and I guess I want to keep you my little boy for as long as possible."

"I know."

"Can I call you Kenny when no one's around?"

"Sure."

"Good night, Kenny."

He kissed her and said, "Good night, Mommy," then looked back and smiled as he walked away.

Angie tried to relax but couldn't. She went in, poured a glass of wine, then returned to her chair on the deck. She took a few sips before her thoughts returned to Harvey. She wondered why she didn't recognize him. *Yes, his hair has receded some and he has a beard, but his broad shoulders, deep voice, and dark sexy eyes are the same.*

One question after another came to mind. She wondered if he had lied about having another girlfriend. And did he act as if he had never been with another girl just to make her comfortable and anxious to be his first? Did he actually join the navy, or was that a maneuver to get her to feel sorry for him and give in to his desires? *What he didn't know was that I wanted him as much as he wanted me, maybe more.*

"I only wish he hadn't lied."

He must've found out about his girlfriend being pregnant soon after being with me. Maybe he thought since he had to get married, it was best to avoid telling me, which would've complicated his life. After all, he didn't know that I was also carrying his son. The way he talks about his wife, he loved her very much. And by not telling her about me, or me about her, probably was best for their marriage.

I wonder if he will deny or admit that Kenny is his son. He probably thinks I will soon recognize him or maybe he thinks I already have. If so, he definitely won't show up tomorrow. More than likely, I'll never see him again.

What a scoundrel I've made him out to be. He may have a good reason for not calling or writing, and I shouldn't judge him until he tells me why—if I ever see him again. I hope I do, and I hope his reason is good.

CHAPTER 24

Angie and Ken had agreed to take *Tooler* out even if Harvey and Rick didn't make it. Ken had *Tooler's* sail cover off, her jib was rigged and ready to be unfurled, and her engine was warming. When he finished preparing *Tooler*, he rushed up the stairs, taking two steps at a time.

"What's ready to take aboard?"

"You certainly are eager."

"When they get here, I want to be ready to leave the dock. It's almost nine, I wonder where they are?"

"You like Rick a lot, don't you?"

"Yes, I do. I like his dad too. I think they're really neat. Don't you?"

"Well, yes. But let's not get our hopes up. Harvey may have changed his mind about buying *Tooler*."

She was trying to prepare him if they didn't show.

"They'll be here."

"What makes you so sure?"

"I just believe they will."

"If not, you won't be too disappointed if we go alone, will you?"

"Oh no. But *Tooler* will be easier to handle if we have some help."

Still trying to prepare him, she said, "If they show, they show, and if not, we'll go without them. Okay?"

"Okay."

Angie was sitting in the cockpit and Ken was pacing the dock. The food was stowed, and they were ready.

"What time is it?" Ken asked.

"Five after nine." She was beginning to feel concern for her son.

"I'll go to the front of the house and wait for them there."

Angie leaned back against the bulkhead and listened to the smooth sound of the engine. She was thinking about her predicament with Harvey and how to resolve it, when she heard, "They're here, Mom.

They're here." She looked at her watch: 9:15. The boys were carrying an ice chest and Harvey was carrying two large bags.

"I'm sorry we're late. I had no idea the traffic on a Sunday morning is that bad." As he talked, she looked into his eyes for any sign of regret or guilt—they only expressed pleasure.

She hoped her eyes didn't reflect her suspicions when she said, "You're not that late. Let me help you with one of those bags."

"Did you bring your bathing suits?" Ken asked.

"Yes," Rick answered.

"Mom said we can go ashore at Egmont, if you have time."

"I love Egmont. Do we have time, Dad?"

"We have all day."

Angie and Harvey looked at each other and smiled. A strange feeling jolted her. He was Skip. It was hard for her to imagine that he was someone she should be upset with.

"Sk…Harvey." *Oh my god! I almost said his name.* "Would you like to take the helm?"

"I'd love to."

She directed him out the canal and into the channel. "The boys and I will hoist the main and let out the jib when you're ready."

He held *Tooler* into the wind and shouted, "Hoist the mainsail!"

When the mainsail was up and secured, Ken went to the cockpit and hauled in and secured the sheet. Harvey let *Tooler* off the wind a little and shouted, "Unfurl the jib!"

Angie and Rick joined Ken in the cockpit and began hauling in the jib sheet while Ken let out the furling line. Harvey pointed *Tooler* in the direction he wanted to sail; Ken turned off the engine and adjusted the sails. Ken continued to fine-tune the sails as *Tooler's* speed increased.

Rick watched what Ken did and helped when he could. "So you and your mom take *Tooler* out alone?"

Ken turned and smiled at his mother. "All the time."

"You guys are good!"

"I agree," Harvey said. "You guys are good."

By the time they anchored off Egmont, it was time for lunch. They sat together in the cockpit while eating the sandwiches Angie had prepared. Angie and Harvey didn't talk much. They didn't need to; the boys kept them entertained with their nonstop talking and laughing. Harvey's many interests and outgoing personality caused Angie to occasionally forget how he had lied and abandoned her. She was actually enjoying his company and found it difficult to remember why she should not. But it was not long before she was back to wondering why he had deceived her.

Ken stood and said to Rick, "Since we're this close to shore, how about instead of inflating the raft, we swim ashore?"

"Sounds good to me."

Ken put the boarding ladder over the side, then he and Rick dove in. They swam back to the boat and Ken asked, "Are you coming?"

Angie answered, "Maybe later."

Harvey watched as they began swimming to shore. "My god, Angela. They look so much alike I can hardly tell them apart."

"They should." She knew as soon as the words left her mouth, she should not have said it and wondered why she did.

He gave her an inquisitive look. "Why did you say that?"

She had started the conversation she had hoped to put off a little longer, but even though she was not prepared, it was too late to stop; she had to continue. "Do you remember making love to a girl thirteen years ago in a rain storm?"

"No, Angela, I don't."

"You can call me Angie." She was hoping that by saying the name he knew her by that night would help him remember.

"No, Angie, I don't remember."

"I think you do remember. You just don't want to admit it."

"You must be mistaken. Let's see. Thirteen years ago, I was married."

"You mean you were married when you were with me!"

"Angie, I have never been with you. Trust me. That's not something I'd forget."

"I don't believe you, Skip."

"Skip. You called me Skip?"

"That's the name you gave me."

"You made love to Skip, and Ken is his son?"

"You aren't Skip?"

"Skip was my brother."

"What do you mean, 'was'?"

He put his face in his hands.

"Oh, Angie. You have no idea how happy you've made me. Ken is Skip's son."

"What did you mean when you said he was your brother?"

"You don't know what happened?"

Her throat was beginning to tighten, and she could hardly get the words out. "No. What happened?"

She anxiously waited while he regained some control of his emotions. "You knew he joined the navy?"

"Yes. I was with him the night before he left."

"Oh my god. You were the Angie he told my wife and me about. God, he loved you."

"I have to know! Please tell me!"

"Two fellows were picking on one. He was trying to break it up when one of the two stabbed him. He died two hours later. That happened the day after he arrived."

Angie's tears began to flow, and she was shaking with emotion. Harvey slid closer to her. They put their arms around each other and cried until their necks were wet with the other's tears. After several minutes, Angie pulled away and, in a voice she could barely control, said, "I feel so guilty. I always thought he lied to me."

"Skip would never do that."

"I know that now."

"Skip and I were closer than most brothers, and it about killed me when he died. Our mother was a poor excuse for a mother. She was an alcoholic, she lied, and she cheated on our father, which caused him to die way before his time. After our father's death, she had a different man in our house almost every night. She embarrassed us around our friends, so we stopped having friends. She wrote worthless checks and owed money to anyone that wasn't smart enough to be conned. That's why to this day, my phone is unlisted. I'm afraid some of her old friends will call looking for money. The mortgage company foreclosed on our house, and since we didn't have any friends or family, we lived on the streets until Skip and I got jobs. For many years, Skip and I only had each other.

"I guess the reason I'm telling you this is to let you know how close we were. I miss him more than you can imagine. But knowing he lives in your son is a wonderful gift. Thanks, Angie."

"You've made me understand that Skip was not the scoundrel I thought he was. Many times, I have thought about my son having the genes of a man who would deceive and lie. I won't be bothered with that thought again."

"The navy sent me his things, and when I unpacked his suitcase, I found a letter he wrote you. It was in an envelope that wasn't addressed. He probably intended to mail it the next day. I'll bring it to you tomorrow."

"Do you mind if I pick it up tonight?"

"Not at all."

"I can hardly wait."

"Our sons are going to see that we've been crying," Harvey said. "What are we going to tell them?"

"The truth."

"The whole truth?"

"The whole truth."

Ken was first up the ladder. He looked at his mother, then Harvey, then back to his mother.

"What's wrong, Mom?"

"Nothing's wrong." She handed each a towel. "Dry off and we'll tell you."

Harvey moved to the seat on the other side; his son sat beside him and Ken sat beside his mother.

Angie put her arm around her son and pulled him close. "When you have asked about your real father, I've always told you that he joined the navy and I never heard from him. Right?"

"Right."

"There's a reason I never heard from him. He was killed trying to help a fellow that was in a fight with two bullies."

"How do you know?"

"He was Harvey's brother."

"How did you find out that my father was Harvey's brother?"

"Your father looked so much like Harvey that I accused him of being your father."

Ken lifted his head. "What was my dad's name?"

Angie answered, "Skip was the only name I knew."

"His name was Charles," Harvey said. "The reason he was called Skip is when we were young, we played in a large wooden box that we pretended to be a boat. He was always the skipper, so I just shortened it to Skip. It stuck, and almost no one knew him by his real name."

"Guess what, Ken?" Rick said.

Using Rick's saying, Ken answered, "I give up."

"That makes us cousins."

As Ken lifted his hand to high-five, he said, "All right!"

They high-fived, then he and his new uncle shook hands and embraced.

There was a favorable wind for smooth sailing with no tacking. Harvey was standing at the helm; the boys had set the sails and were sitting on the deck, side by side, looking forward, with their backs resting against the front of the cabin. Angie was sitting with her back against the bulkhead, admiring Harvey. He looked so proud and in control as he held the wheel and watched the sails.

The emotion Harvey had expressed while telling her what happened to his brother was still clear and a good indication to her that he was a man that loved forever. Occasionally, while admiring him, he glanced at her. They smiled each time their eyes met, and she was finding it difficult to keep her eyes off his. She had to go to him.

She stood, and before joining him behind the helm, she glanced at the boys; they were looking forward. She put her arm around his waist and kissed him on the cheek. "I'm sorry I was mean to you."

He chuckled. "You weren't mean to me."

"I shouldn't have accused you of being Skip, and I shouldn't have doubted Skip's sincerity. And instead of being hurt and feeling sorry for myself, I should've invested more time and effort in locating him."

He put his arm around her, and she melted in his embrace. He slowly turned his face to hers and gently kissed her waiting lips. "I'm sure you did the best you could." They were silent for several minutes. "That's all behind us, and there's nothing we can do about the past." He paused for a moment. "Can you believe how this all came about? All from your ad to sell *Tooler*. Do you believe in fate?"

"Yes, I do. I also know the boat you and Skip owned was named *Fate*."

"He told you about *Fate*?"

"Yes. I could tell he really loved her."

"I still have her."

"You do!"

"Oh, yes. I will never sell her. She holds too many treasured memories. Maybe someday, Rick, and now Ken, will have their own cherished memories aboard *Fate*. I hope it's all right with you if I include Ken in my and Rick's life."

"Only if I'm included."

He pulled her closer and kissed her hair. "You are."

"Then *Tooler* is no longer for sale."

"Good. I hope that means what I think it does."

"It does."